APPLE SEEDS &
MURDEROUS DEEDS

A FIONA MCCABE MYSTERY

KATHY CRANSTON

CHAPTER 1

"Anyone would think the Celtic Tiger was beating down your door," Gerry Reynolds said with a snort. "A cocktail bar in Ballycashel. Lord bless us and save us."

Fiona McCabe glanced up from the magazine she'd been reading under the bar. She forced a smile. Gerry had been coming to McCabe's at least once a week since she reopened the family pub three months before. Their conversations ran like clockwork. She closed her magazine and tried not to smile as she predicted his next words.

I don't suppose you have a pint of Guinness for a hardworking man.

"I don't suppose you have a pint of Guinness for a hardworking man," he said, rolling up his newspaper and dropping it on the bar. The racing pages faced up, messily scrawled with blue ink.

The irony was that Gerry hadn't done an honest day's work in his life—not that Fiona had any intention of pointing that out.

"We don't have Guinness on tap, I'm afraid,' Fiona said, as apologetic as she had been the last five times he'd asked.

His eyes widened. "What? No Guinness? But sure this is Francis McCabe's place. You can't have done away with the Guinness."

She shrugged. "I've got a craft stout that you might like?"

He stared at her, unblinking. She offered him something different every time and always got the same response. He shook his head. "I'll have a Guinness."

She sighed. "Well, I have a few cans here. Won't be the same as a pint but I can pour you one if you like."

An aul can…

"An aul can?" he said, looking at her incredulously. "Sure I could get one of them from the shop."

"You could," she said, not unkindly. "I said it before—I'm trying something new. Sure there're already five pubs in town and the only reason Dad closed this place was because the crowds were thinning."

"So you turn the place into a hipster spot?" he said, as if that was the most heinous crime he'd ever heard of.

Fiona cringed. "No. Not at all." She sighed. What was the point of explaining her theory to a man whose area of expertise was five-finger discounts and knowing how many robberies you could get away with before they'd hit you with a custodial sentence?

The truth was, she'd decided to do something a little different. When the economy was booming, developers had been crawling all over themselves to build new estates in every small town in Ireland, including Ballycashel. Those estates had now been empty for years, but signs of life were starting to emerge as young first-time buyers were priced out of Dublin's soaring market. She had taken a gamble; changed things up and hoped to attract a different market to the other traditional pubs around town.

"I don't see why you have to cater to the posh crowd. What's wrong with a pint of Guinness and a roaring fire?"

"Nothing at all," Fiona said wearily. "I used to love that when I was home for the weekend and the weather was miserable. But there isn't enough business for two pubs in Ballycashel anymore, never mind six."

"Your father must be turning in his grave."

She snorted. "I'll tell him you said that."

"Do, aye."

"I don't think he gets it," said a voice from the other end of the bar. "*Gerard*, you only say that about people who are *dead*."

Fiona smiled warily. "Are you alright for a drink there, Dec?" She wished he hadn't said anything. Most people in the town knew better than to get into an argument with Gerry Reynolds.

Sure enough, Gerry tilted his head to one side and looked at Dec as if he'd been gravely insulted. Next thing Fiona knew, he was picking up his paper and moving along the bar with the menace of an apex predator.

"I don't want any trouble," Fiona warned in the sternest voice she could muster. Indeed, that was one of the benefits of running a cocktail bar slash coffee shop: she didn't have to throw people out of the bar very often. The local hardcases—Gerry excluded—tended to stay away from places where the drinks came in oddly shaped glasses and candy colours.

"Neither do I," Gerry hissed through the gap in his front teeth. He came to a stop beside Dec. "Here, what did you just say to me?"

Dec looked up in that slow way of his. Fiona remembered it well: he had been close to her brother Colm way back when they were all in primary school. And then there was her own—brief—history with him.

"I was just trying to help you out. You misused the phrase."

"Is that so?" Gerry asked, voice dangerously quiet. He attempted to stand straighter and failed on account of the skin-full he'd probably had earlier in Phelan's. It didn't make him any less intimidating.

Gerry was one of the local hard nuts—always in trouble of one kind or another. Fiona had never had any trouble with him herself, but she had heard plenty of stories about him. He was not the kind of guy you rubbed up the wrong way if you could help it.

"It is," Dec said, not taking his eyes off the other man.

Fiona sent him a silent plea, but he kept his focus on Reynolds.

Gerry laughed, but his eyes remained as cold and blank as ever. "We have a tough guy, ha? What happened? You did your time and now you've gone from a choir boy to a big tough gangster?"

Dec rolled his eyes. "I didn't say that, you did. Will you let me drink my drink in peace?"

"What on earth is that muck you're drinking?" Gerry said, reaching over his shoulder and picking up the bottle.

Behind the bar, Fiona jabbed a little button under the counter twice in rapid succession. She looked around the bar, desperately hoping there was someone who could get Gerry under control. There was no one—apart from Gerry and Dec at the bar, there were just a couple of students who must have been on college holidays; Tony Morris and a friend of his, whom Fiona had never met. Mrs Finnegan sat in the corner nursing a brandy as she chatted to Mrs Roche, but they wouldn't be much good in a bar brawl unless it involved knitting needles or mass booklets.

"Look lads, calm down. It's Thursday evening. The week is nearly done. Let's enjoy a quiet drink, yeah? Gerry, I'll get you a Guinness—you can pretend it's draught."

Nobody in town would choose a can of Guinness when they could walk a hundred yards down the road and get a perfect creamy pint in Phelan's, but that wasn't the point. Fiona kept them there as a fall-back option for when people really wanted a pint.

Now she wished she'd just kept the kegs in. She'd do anything to keep Gerry placated. She was more worried about Dec than herself. he'd been through enough in the past year without Gerry causing more trouble for him.

But Gerry wasn't sold on the idea. "If I wanted a *can*, I'd have gone to the *shop*," he slurred, looking so pleased that Fiona doubted he remembered saying the same thing just moments before. "Gimme a Jameson."

She paused, staring at the door. She was okay with the idea of giving him a stout if it meant he'd calm down, but she had no intention of feeding him spirits. If the Gardaí arrived, it might cause her to lose her licence: Sergeant Brennan wouldn't miss an opportunity like that.

Before Gerry could react, Marty McCabe came storming through the door, hurley in hand. Fiona felt giddy with relief. She nodded her thanks to her brother and jerked her head as subtly as she could in Gerry's direction—not that Marty needed the hint.

"Gerard," Marty said, moving across the room at a speed that seemed impossible for someone of his size.

Fiona's eldest brother was built like a tank from his years in the army. He still ran five miles a day and had set up a weights room in the semi-detached house he shared with their brother Colm.

Gerry took one glance at Marty and another at the hurley. He had seen Marty on the field and was all too aware the damage he could cause with that thing.

"I'll be going, so," he muttered, not looking at any them.

"Thanks, Marty," Fiona said with a sigh of relief as the door swung closed and the bar's patrons returned their attention to their drinks. "He's normally grand, but I was worried he was going to start kicking off."

"Sorry," Dec said, holding up his hand. "It was me that set him off."

"What possessed you, Dec? I mean, you know how he gets; everyone from around here knows that."

Dec shrugged sullenly. "I just got mad listening to him droning on, Fi. The state of him—the way he struts around the town as if he's a tough guy. Well, I'll tell ye for nothing: he wouldn't hold a candle to some of the nutcases I've seen in…" his face fell as he trailed off.

Fiona glanced at her brother quickly before turning her attention back to Dec. "Sorry, Dec. I didn't mean to nag you."

"Ah you weren't," he said, waving his hand. "And I don't want you tiptoeing around me because I've been to jail."

She shook her head. "You're right. Ah, I wasn't. We just… Everyone around here was rooting for you, Dec. It wasn't right you getting sent away like that."

Martin nodded and clapped a huge hand on Dec's shoulder. "She's right. Mam and some of her friends went and protested outside Garda headquarters, for all the good it did."

Dec looked stunned. "Ye let them do that? Sure that'd only give Brennan ammo to use against them. He's out of control."

Fiona sighed. "We tried to stop them, but there was no talking to them. You have people looking out for you here—remember that."

Dec looked at each of them in turn and smiled. "Thanks, lads. It means a lot. Sure I'm out now. Ready to get on with my life."

Fiona stole a look at her brother when Dec was busy with his drink. His expression was serious, which was definitely not normal for Marty McCabe. She suspected she knew why: if Declan Hanlon thought he was getting a fresh start now, he had another thing coming. Sergeant Brennan didn't let go of a grudge in a hurry and Dec had obviously rubbed him up the wrong way. It was the only explanation for Dec's incarceration for not paying his TV licence when there were real criminals roaming the streets—and the pubs.

CHAPTER 2

"Dec Hanlon was in earlier," Fiona said as soon as there was a lull in the conversation.

Conversational lulls didn't often happen in the McCabe household: six of the seven children still lived around town, and Margaret McCabe insisted on cooking dinner for them all as often as possible.

"Oh right," her father said, pursing his lips and taking the dish of carrots from one of his sons.

Mr McCabe had never warmed to Dec, mainly because of the innocent flirtation that had taken place between Dec and Fiona when he was in third year and she was in second. Never mind that the relationship had lasted a grand total of three weeks, nor that it was over a decade in the past; Francis McCabe couldn't stand the sight of the man who had had the utter cheek to try and woo his favourite daughter.

"Oh come on, Francis," his wife said. Everyone called him Francis, even his wife and close friends. He was just one of those characters for whom a nickname would have seemed strange. "He's a good boy. Sure wouldn't you welcome him with open arms if he called over and asked to take our Fi out?"

Fiona groaned. "Mam, I'm nearly thirty. Don't you think he'd be asking me rather than coming here and asking you and Dad?"

Francis McCabe grunted. "He wouldn't have the bottle. I'd send him packing, so I would."

"Jesus, Mary and Joseph," Mrs McCabe said with a heavy sigh. "Sure no one's good enough for her according to you. She'll die a spinster!"

"Mam!" Fiona yelled and her sister Kate yelled in unison. Kate was going through a single patch and had taken to defending Fiona during the all-too-regular interrogation sessions about her relationship status.

"Yeah, leave her alone, Mam," Marty said quietly. "She can't find a fella around the town who'll take her. It's not her fault."

"You're all a bunch of absolute—"

"Language!"

"I said nothing!"

"You were about to!"

Fiona pushed her plate away and put her head down on her outstretched hands. She was too tired for their usual nonsense. She'd taken to opening the bar at seven in the morning to try and attract the few commuters who had actually moved to Ballycashel, but foot traffic was still relatively quiet. Still, business was improving—one day soon she hoped to be able to afford to hire someone to help. It helped that she lived right upstairs from the bar too: it was easy to open early and then shut down for a few hours until the afternoon.

"Look, I appreciate that we have our strange dysfunctional situation here, but for once can we just sit around the table and talk about our days? Like normal people? I'm sick of ye all ganging up and slagging me. I could have cooked dinner for myself in the flat instead of coming around here."

Mrs McCabe cried out as if she'd been struck. She clasped a hand over her chest. "Fiona Mary McCabe! Well I never! How could you be so ungrateful? After I slaving over the cooker all day to make you a healthy dinner? You wouldn't eat your vegetables otherwise."

"I don't think spuds count as veggies, Mam," Kate said mournfully.

"Sure haven't ye peas?"

"Pure sugar," Kate shot back.

Sensing a war was brewing and being in no mood to return to her dark, empty flat, Fiona held her hands up. "Enough!" she shouted. "We're starting again. Rewind. Marty, how was your day?"

"Oh it was lovely, thank you Fiona. Mrs O'Hagan was in earlier and I helped her pick out some new tiles for the fireplace in the front room. Her Nina is due back from Australia for a holiday so she's keen to spruce the place up. Then we had Father Jimmy in." Marty paused and threw his eyes skyward. "Couldn't get rid of the fella. He stood there blustering at me for a good half an hour, berating the people who get the offertory collection envelopes and then have the cheek not to use them. You'd swear he was penniless the way he goes on. Never mind that he has more money than anyone else in the town."

"That's no way to talk about a priest," their mother interrupted.

"Don't get me started," Marty said. "Jail'd be the best place for him—not the parish house."

Mrs McCabe sucked in a breath. "You saw Dec—I forgot with all of your fighting," she said, not mentioning that she was one of the chief instigators. "Well, did he tell you much?"

Marty answered before Fi could. "No. Sure it wasn't like we could ask him. He seems cut up about the whole thing—it was written all over his face."

"Oh," said his mother. "You were there too? What, did ye all head off for lunch without me?"

"No, Mam," Fiona sighed. She paused. Her parents hated the thought of her working in the bar alone, no matter that her scant clientele was a whole lot safer than that of your average pub. She had never told them about Gerry's regular but brief visits, because he had never caused trouble before and she hadn't wanted to worry them. It had been her father's idea to run a cable between the bar and the hardware shop next door so Fiona had a direct alarm bell to her oldest brother if she ever needed it. She normally only used it to get him over for a chat and a cup of tea when the afternoons were quiet. Neither of them had bothered to point out to their parents that the hardware shop was normally closed by seven in the evening, and Marty was long gone on weekend nights when trouble was most likely to start.

But Mrs McCabe would not be put off. "Well?" she said. "You didn't think to invite me and I cooped up here all on my own not even half a mile away?"

"He was in the bar, Mam." She glanced down at the table. "Gerry Reynolds came in mouthing off and I used the bell to get Marty over."

"Oh my Lord!"

"No, Mam, there's no need to worry. Listen!"

Mrs McCabe had gone pale and was clutching her husband's arm with such force that her knuckles had turned white.

"Mam!" Marty said sharply. "It was fine. He's all talk—you know that. As soon as he saw me come in with the hurley…"

"Oh, Martin!" she cried. "You brought a hurley! Sure what if he took it off you and used it against you?"

No one around the table could keep a straight face.

"Why are ye all laughing at me? Amn't I only concerned for my firstborn?"

"Mam," Kate said quietly, finally looking up from her phone. "Marty's six-five and built like a brick—"

"Language!"

"I said nothing! All I was saying was Marty's built like a tank and Gerry Reynolds spends all his time in the betting shop or in the chipper. He'd only hurt Marty if he sat on him and I don't think that's about to happen."

"I don't like that character," Francis McCabe said, forking a lump of boiled potato.

It was a wonder any of them managed to eat at these family dinners, Fiona thought, for the amount of talking they did—usually all at the same time.

"Like I said, he's never caused trouble before. He was giving me lip and Dec called him up on it. He zeroed in on Dec then; started giving him a hard time about how he's the big hardman now."

"Dec did seem different," Marty said through a mouthful of roast beef.

Fiona shook her head. She didn't want to admit it, but there was no denying it. Three months in jail had changed Dec Hanlon from cheeky and happy-go-lucky to sullen and serious. She had seen it in his eyes.

"Maybe he's still catching up on sleep and getting used to being out," she offered.

"Nah," Ben said. "He's been out a good while now. I've seen him around town. Barely said two words to me. Sounds like he's mad to get away from here."

Fiona sighed. "And all because of Sergeant Brennan."

"Robocop," her father said automatically.

Fiona had given him that name and it had stuck—at least within the walls of the McCabe household. None of them was foolish enough to call him that to his face—they had seen what happened to those who angered Sergeant Brennan.

"I don't understand why nobody reports him," Ben said. "They must have HR policies that prevent behaviour like that. He's a bully."

"Ah, sure," Francis said, rolling his eyes. "I'm sure they do. But which unfortunate is going to take a case against the son of one of the Garda Commissioner's closest friends?"

It was true. Fiona had discovered the link long before Alex Brennan descended on Ballycashel and began his iron reign. No one in her family knew how she had learnt the truth—and she wanted to keep it that way.

"Oh and we went and protested, Francis. Brennan could have me in jail next!"

"But you knew all about his connections, Margaret," her husband said. "We all tried to tell you, but there was no stopping you."

She sighed. "Ah, it was for poor Declan. What were we supposed to do? Quake in our boots? No, we needed to have our voices heard—for all the good it did us. Will you visit me when he finds a way to throw me in the women's prison?"

Fiona rolled her eyes. Her mother was well known around town for her dramatics.

"Never, Mammy," Ben said. He was the youngest boy and his mother's clear favourite, though she denied it to the hilt. "Sure you can't keep a good woman down—they'd have to release you."

Fiona expected the others to jump in and protest that her mother was being overly-dramatic, but nobody did. She knew Sergeant Brennan better than any of them—not that she could let them know that.

"Do you really think he's capable of throwing her in jail because she protested against him?"

Her father lowered his paper and looked at her as if she was mad. "There's no love lost between me and Declan Hanlon, I'll tell you that for nothing. But when you think about what they put him in for... I don't know who's safe around here anymore." He turned to his wife and smiled. "Don't worry, love. If you do get sent to jail I'll take you up some of those magazines you like."

CHAPTER 3

The next day was Friday, meaning Fiona had no chance of getting away early for family dinner. She was thankful for it too. She hadn't gotten back to the flat until well after eleven the night before and there had been no let up in their fussing. The last thing her mother said to her on the way out was that she'd never be able to sleep knowing Fiona was spending her evenings alone in that bar.

She glanced around. Things were picking up. Of course, a relatively busy evening for McCabe's meant a small handful of customers instead of none. Her mother had nothing to worry about, as she had tried to explain the night before.

"You look very deep in thought."

Fiona smiled. Dec was sitting on the same bar stool as he had occupied the previous evening. "Ah, just daydreaming. It's good that you're getting out and about," she blurted, not able to think of anything else to say. She immediately cringed. "Sorry, I didn't mean to be awkward—words just seem to shoot out of my mouth without me having any control over them."

He looked amused. "I know. You've always been like that. You're grand—I'm not offended."

"That's good," she whispered. "I mean it. Good that you're not letting it get you down. I suppose coming to a bar is the biggest challenge. Hopefully we'll see you around here more often now."

He flushed the colour of beetroot. "To be honest, Fi, I couldn't face seeing all the aul boys in Phelan's."

She tried not to laugh. Fiona was long past the point of being offended when people chose to avoid her bar in favour of one of the more traditional pubs in the town. "Fair enough," she admitted. "You're not the only one. I should market this place to the new age crowd for the solitude. Meditation and margaritas."

"I thought that shower didn't drink? You'd have to change your food as well." He pointed to a spot over her head. "No more meat or cheese. Or anything nice, really."

Fiona rolled her eyes. "No way am I changing it up to offer lettuce burgers and quinoa bowls. Are you hungry?"

"No."

"Are you sure? How about some Turkish bread and hummus? Both made fresh this morning."

"No thanks," he smiled.

"Are you sure? They're really good, if I do say so myself."

He laughed. "I said I was fine! Just because I mentioned food doesn't mean I'm starving. You're turning into a feeder, just like your mother."

Fiona gasped in mock outrage. "How could you say a thing like that? Of all the things to say to a woman. It's charm school they should have sent you to, not jail."

He threw his head back and laughed. "God it feels good to have someone say that word without apologising and getting all awkward." He shook his head and reached over to the little box on the bar. "What are these?"

Fiona sighed. "You'll get a great laugh out of this. They're matchbooks. I thought they'd give the place a retro feel. You know, people write their phone numbers on there to give to someone they like."

He frowned, running the little folder of cardboard through his fingers and staring at it. "Why would you do that, though? Would you not just put your number in their phone?"

"Practical, Dec," Fi conceded. Her siblings had said pretty much the same thing.

"Sure what do I know?" he said, shrugging and putting it down beside his drink. "You're ahead of your time, Fi McCabe. They'll be down here begging you to open a branch in Ballyjamesduff and Tullamore in no time. You'll be a cocktail bar tycoon."

She snorted with laughter. "Yeah right! Can you imagine? I'll get really full of myself and start wearing a fedora with a feather in it and some kind of cape and—"

"Excuse me?"

Fiona spun around and came face-to-face with a man she had never seen before. He was dressed all in black with the exception of his tortoise shell glasses. He reminded her of a college professor.

"Can I get some service here?"

"Sorry," she smiled. "I didn't see you there. What can I get you?"

He rolled his eyes. "If you had bothered to *look* then I'm sure you would have seen me."

"Fair point," she said. "What can I get you?"

"I'll have a gin and tonic," he said with a pinched expression.

"Sorry, I'm all out."

He seemed affronted. "All out of gin? Or is it tonic? Not both, heaven forbid. This is a bar—correct

"I'm out of gin. The supplier was supposed to come yesterday but he never showed. I can make you something else, but it'd have to be with another spirit."

"What kind of bar runs out of gin?"

"This one, I suppose. Is there anything else I can get for you?"

He didn't respond. She turned and looked up to see what had riled him now. She was surprised to find him staring intently at Dec.

"It's yourself," he said, as if he was remarking on the weather.

"It sure is," Dec said, taking a long swig of his drink.

"Let me buy you a drink," the stranger said, moving around the bar unbidden and taking a seat next to Dec.

Fiona looked warily at her old friend, wondering what on earth was going on. To her surprise, though, Dec didn't bat an eyelid. She wondered if he knew the guy. Maybe Dec had gotten used to people recognising him as the fella who'd gone to jail. She frowned. But this man wasn't a local. And cases like Dec's—however unjust—didn't make the national news.

"How about a…" the man squinted at the array of bottles behind her. "A spiced rum and coke? Can you manage that?"

Fiona forgot her curiosity and turned so the stranger wouldn't see the expression on her face. "Sure, I can do that."

"Well that's reassuring," the man replied in the same obnoxious tone.

"Yeah, go on so," Dec said. "I'll have the same."

Fiona felt confident she'd lose the plot if the man made one more snarky comment. She moved around the bar to clean up the few tables that had been used that day, telling herself the customer was always right.

CHAPTER 4

The two men were still deep in conversation when Fiona returned to the bar. Things were getting busier—there were a few customers waiting at the bar.

"What can I get you?" she asked Will Connolly.

"A pint… I mean a bottle of…" he squinted to see in the fridges behind her. "Is that Richer's pale ale?"

She nodded.

"I'll have one of those please."

"How's the business going?" she asked, turning to retrieve the bottle from the fridge. "If you ever decide to turn some of those apples into cider let me know—I'm always looking for new local producers I can stock."

He laughed. "I wish. It's hard enough finding the time to get everything picked and packed and shipped off. Though cider production might be better paid than selling to the supermarkets, that's for sure."

"Worth a thought, Will. Those guys who set up Abbott's Ale are doing really well—they're supplying loads of bars now."

"Aye, I heard that." He turned and stared down the bar. "Who's your man with Hanlon?"

She shrugged. "No idea. I've never seen him before."

"They look pally."

They did, now that she thought about it. The strange man hadn't introduced himself to Dec, so she would have assumed Dec knew him if it wasn't for the fact that he paid the man no heed until he spoke first. Maybe, she thought, Dec had been too busy chatting to notice him.

She handed Will his beer and glanced at the door when the bell went off. It was an old-fashioned touch—her family had had a great laugh—but it was something Fi wouldn't be without. It stopped people sneaking in or out without her noticing if she had her back to the bar. She couldn't remember seeing Dec's friend come in, but put it down to having been too distracted by their conversation.

Gerry Reynolds sauntered in the door and looked around as if he owned the place. A chill ran down her spine as she thought of something that had struck her late the night before. What if Gerry was after money? She had no idea what business he was in—town gossip had him involved in a range of nefarious activities from robbery to betting rings. What if he had a protection racket going too? She could barely afford the overheads as it was without handing money over to Gerry—in fact, she'd rather shut down for good before she did that.

"Evening, Gerry," she said with a nod, forcing herself to sound cheerful. There was no way she was going to let him see she was intimidated.

He turned and did a double take, as if he was surprised to see her there. "And what kind of a place do you call this? Is it Dublin we're in?"

She resisted the urge to roll her eyes. Was he going to start making his weekly visits more frequent? She wasn't sure she could handle the stale jokes. Instead of saying that, though, she simply shrugged. "Don't I wish. Might have enough money to pay the power bill if that was the case."

He moved closer to the bar, eyes narrowed. "Sure isn't there loads of money in pubs? You'll have the mattress above stuffed full of fifty euro notes."

Fiona's blood ran cold. She could see in her peripheral vision that there was no one close enough to be in earshot. She swallowed. "I wish, Gerry. Maybe in dreamworld. What can I get you?"

"I'll have a pint of Guinness, love."

Fiona smiled and resisted the urge to look around for the hidden cameras. Sometimes she felt like that was the only explanation for some of the goings on in her bar—her family had called in the telly people and told them to mess with her for the nation's entertainment. But she doubted that was the case now—no TV producer in their right mind would put Gerry Reynolds on the telly.

**

While Gerry was deliberating over the drinks menu, the door opened again. Fiona looked around to see who it was. She didn't think she had ever seen the place this busy, not even in the leadup to Christmas, when the local lads on their Twelve Pubs of Christmas had no choice but to call into her bar or be forced to drive even further out of town to complete their dozen.

Mary and Pete Prendergast shuffled through the door and over to the closest unoccupied table. Pete returned to the bar as Mary shrugged off her coat and made herself comfortable.

"Howaya Fiona," Pete nodded. "How's life treating you?"

"Ah, not too bad, not too bad," she smiled. "And yourself?"

He winced and Fiona took that as a bad sign. Pete Prendergast never missed a chance to complain about the various things that were weighing on his mind.

In the last few months alone he had suffered from a terrible earache, insomnia, trouble with creditors and a run-in with the revenue department. Fiona looked around, desperately hoping that one of the other customers would down their drink and hurry to the bar for another.

"Ah, well, now," he said, taking a slow breath in as if it pained him to do so. "I was grand until Wednesday. Finally getting me health back. And then you wouldn't believe what—"

Fiona glanced up, curious as to why he'd stopped talking so abruptly. She found him staring down the bar at Dec and the stranger. All of the colour had seeped from his face.

"Pete?" she asked, frowning. "Is everything alright?"

She began to feel guilty for being so easily irritated: he looked truly stricken.

"Pete?" she asked again when he gave no indication of having heard her the first time.

He looked at her quickly as if she had disturbed him from a dream. "Yeah?" he said.

Fiona frowned. She had never seen anyone look so harassed or hunted. "You started to say something but you trailed off there." She never expected to find herself prompting Pete to tell one of his stories, but something was really wrong here.

He shook his head and waved his hand. "Ah, nothing. Here, I'll be back in a minute—I just need to talk to Mary."

He hurried to the table and whispered something to his wife. Mary glanced back at the bar—Fiona looked away before she could catch the look on the woman's face. She would kick herself for doing so later, but at the time she didn't want to seem nosy.

Within two minutes, Mary and Pete had stood and hurried from the bar. They were so quiet that Fiona was sure she wouldn't have noticed them go if it wasn't for her trusty bell above the door.

She glanced along the bar and saw that Dec was still deep in conversation with the man. They had barely touched their drinks. She moved past them and stood in front of Gerry. That encounter with Pete had rattled her and she felt the need to talk to someone—anyone.

"Have you decided, Gerry?" she asked, grabbing a cloth and wiping the bar as she waited for him to answer. Oh, it'd be some smart comment about her bar no doubt, but at least he wasn't causing trouble with any of her other customers.

He looked up and frowned at her. "Who's your man with the glasses?"

She looked around the bar and almost leapt out of her skin when she saw Mrs Flannery. The old woman made no attempt to hide the fact that she was glaring at Dec. Fiona had never seen the pleasant octogenarian look so furious.

"Well," Gerry demanded.

Fiona started, barely paying attention so transfixed was she by Mrs Flannery. She looked around.

"That's Noel Cassidy," she said. "His family moved into one of the new houses there about five years ago. He's a good lad—did his Leaving Cert there last year." She knew because he'd come in with his CV and asked her if there were any jobs going. She'd had to turn him away, but the upshot was Marty had found some work for him in the hardware shop. He was a good lad with a good head on his shoulders.

"No," Gerry barked. "I know who Noel is. I live here, don't I? No, I mean the other guy."

"Who?"

"Your man with that jailbird friend of yours."

"If *one* more person asks me that..." she started, before stopping abruptly mid-sentence. *Now's not the time to get snarky, Fi; not with hard-nut Gerry on the loose in here. Cop on.* She forced a smile. "I don't know. I've never seen him before in my life."

Gerry pursed his lips, still staring at the man who didn't seem to notice he had become the centre of attention in the bar. "Do you think he's a nark?" he leant against the bar, frowning. "That's what it is, isn't it? Hanlon got out early by singing like a canary."

This time Fi couldn't hold back her laughter. "Oh come on, Gerry. Next thing you'll be telling me you saw Tony Soprano hanging around with his mates outside the butcher's. This is Ballycashel."

His eyes narrowed and she watched him carefully. Gerry Reynolds wasn't the kind of guy you wanted to annoy; not if you could help it. It had been so ridiculous that she hadn't been able to resist, but what if Gerry wasn't just a wannabe thug? What if he was one of those gangster guys from the telly; all ruthless fury behind their tracksuits and runners?

To her relief, his features relaxed and his lips seemed to twist into a smile. At least, that's what Fiona thought it looked like—there was no way to be sure underneath the luxuriant moustache that was his trademark around the town.

"That's funny," he said after a while. "You're funny. Ah, great show that. That Soprano fella was a pure genius."

This time Fiona had more control over herself. "I suppose you could say that, yeah," she managed, before biting her cheek and turning to focus on the already meticulously arranged spirit bottles.

***

When she was finished, she noticed with alarm that Dec's strange companion had gone to the toilet and Gerry was now sitting in the free stool beside Dec. She stood watching them, hand hovering towards the button under the counter. Of course, the flaw in their system was that Marty usually closed the hardware shop at six or seven. They had never given it much thought seeing as the whole thing had been designed to keep her parents happy rather than as a foolproof security system.

She watched them for a few moments, ears perked to hear any raised voices. She reached over past the bowl of quartered lemons and pulled her smartphone closer.

She swiped to unlock the screen, tapped 1-1-2 and paused. Rolling her eyes when she realised she had no other choice, she cleared the screen and instead scrolled through her contacts until she came to the entry for Ballycashel Garda station. She couldn't exactly call the national emergency number and tell them Gerry Reynolds was going off, but one mention of his name to the Gardaí in Ballycashel and there'd be someone over within minutes. How effective they'd be at stifling any trouble was another story.

Fiona was just about to sneak into the tiny office and call the guards when Gerry stood abruptly and stormed from the bar without so much as a nod in her direction. She stared after him before turning to Dec.

"What was that all about? What did he say to you?"

But Dec was uncharacteristically closed off about the encounter. And before she could push the matter, the doors opened and a group of young women walked in, all decked out in pink sashes and tiaras. They might as well have rang a gong and yelled 'ding-ding-ding' as far as Fiona was concerned: hen parties were big business and they didn't often venture to Ballycashel. Fiona plastered on her widest smile and moved to where they were clustering.

"Hello, ladies! Where's the blushing bride? Ah, how could I miss you with those furry handcuffs and obscene toys? Let me get you a Baby Guinness on the house; get the party started."

CHAPTER 5

Mrs McCabe wasn't just revered in her family for her roast dinners. She cooked a top-notch Full Irish breakfast too. Fiona was in dire need of it that morning. The hen party had been a good bunch of girls and she had found herself enjoying the craic and joining them in a round of shots too many. Coupled with the fact that she'd eaten nothing but a cheese toastie all day meant she was suffering the ill-effects now.

"That's one way to drive your own bar into the ground," her father said without lowering the day's paper from his eyes.

"What is, Dad?" she asked, voice hoarse and low like a fifties screen siren.

"Drinking your own profits," he muttered.

"I'm not drinking my profits," she protested weakly. "It was a hen party. I had a few shots with them to get the buzz going. My takings from last night were more than the previous two weeks combined. And that's accounting for the three or four shots I had myself. How do you know anyway? You've had that paper glued to your face since I came in."

"I can smell it," he said, shuffling the paper closed and karate chopping it in the middle to fold it. "And the voice on you. You sound like those ones on the 1580 phone lines."

Across the table, Ben snorted. "You're a fan of them, Dad? I have to say, I'm surprised. I thought you were a man of better moral fibre than that."

Fiona laughed. "Does Mammy know?"

"Ah, lookit," Francis snapped, reaching in the pocket of his dressing gown for his phone. The kids had chipped in and got him an iPhone 6 for Christmas and though he lamented it frequently, he was hardly ever off it. "I've seen the ads. I was only making an observation. An assumption. Ye can check the phone bill if ye want."

Ben glanced at Fiona and shook his head ruefully. "Probably rings them on the mobile so we can't trace it."

"Would ye stop!" Francis bellowed.

The table fell silent. Their father was notorious for not being able to take a slagging and they knew when to stop pushing him.

Fiona leant her head back against the wooden chair and indulged in a fantasy where she left the bar closed for the rest of the day and curled up on the couch watching old movies with Rex, the family dog. It was far too tempting. She had already opened the bar at seven that morning and made coffee for the handful of people who came in at that hour. Business was definitely up since she had started baking scones to display in baskets on the bar, but it was hardly booming.

"That smells divine, Mam," Fiona said, trying to stop her mouth from watering. She couldn't remember the last time she had called over for breakfast—there was always something else to be doing around the bar.

"You'd hope so," Mrs McCabe said, carrying two heaped plates out to the table and then disappearing back to the kitchen for more. "I've been slaving over the cooker for hours."

Fiona felt a twinge of guilt. "Ah, sorry, Mam. I offered to help and you said you were grand."

"Don't mind her," Francis said without looking up from his phone. "I told her I'd be happy with porridge and she looked like she was about to have a heart attack."

"Sure I was worried about my good saucepans. You'd burn the bottom out of them sooner than you'd stir anything." She dropped another two plates on the table. "He's always stuck on that phone," she muttered as she walked away.

Silence descended over them once all six of them had plates in front of them. The table was usually more crowded, but Colm and Enda had been browbeaten into escorting their granny and a group of local pensioners on their annual pilgrimage to Lourdes.

Fiona stared at the plate wondering what to try first. It was heaped high with rashers, sausages, black and white pudding, beans, grilled tomatoes and mushrooms, and Mrs McCabe's hash browns. She had fallen in love with the American diner variety the first time she went to visit Mike in Philadelphia. Fiona had never been to the States, but when she did visit she'd be getting the name of that diner and going there to thank them for their contribution to the McCabe family's wellness (and waistlines).

"Tell me you don't make these from scratch every morning," Fiona said, scooping up another forkful and carefully pressing it against the yolk of one of the perfectly fried eggs. The oozing yolk made her feel a little queasy once more.

"Would you go way outta that! Do you think I'm made of time and chained to the kitchen?"

Fiona froze, fork hovering mid-air over her plate. "Well, you're always telling us how bored you are and I've rarely seen you out of the kitchen."

Mrs McCabe threw her head back and sighed as if she was in pain.

"You asked!" Fiona cried. "Didn't she?" She looked around at her siblings and father for support, but found none. They were all too busy eating and her father was hunched over, staring at his phone.

"He's seriously never off that thing, is he?" she asked, realising that the only way she was going to get out it was to direct her mother's hostility at someone else.

"Tell me about it," her mother said, still frosty. A moment later, though, she leant forward, unable to resist the urge to have a dig at him. "At least he turned it on silent, though. For a few weeks there, all you could hear was the national anthem every time he got a text message."

Ben laughed. "Sure who would the aul boy be texting?"

"They're all at it," Mrs McCabe said with a shrug. "Him and the lads, texting each other night and day about the horses and the dogs and the state of the economy and God knows what else." Her eyes narrowed as Ben's words sunk in. "Why? What's so strange about him texting? I hope you're not suggesting that we're too old."

Fiona smiled serenely at her brother's discomfort. There was one cardinal rule in their house: never make any reference whatsoever to their mother's age. They would never have even known it if it wasn't for the time that Kate was rooting in their parents' wardrobe and came across the marriage certificate, complete with that secret date of birth. Kate had made the mistake of telling their aunt Philomena about it. Mrs McCabe hadn't forgiven them for months.

Their father, of course, couldn't care less about his age. They'd been referring to him as the auld boy since way back when he must have only been in his forties.

No, Ben's problem was that he mentioned his father's age in front of his mother, who happened to be eight months older than her husband (something which had scandalised and shocked the McCabe children on that rainy day in the nineties).

"Ah, Mam, I wasn't talking about you. It was him."

Mrs McCabe wasn't having a bar of it. "You call him old, you call me old."

"Ah, now, lookit," Ben said, clearly not so worried that he couldn't find the time to pause and polish off another slice of toast. "What's age only a number? If I was to meet the two of ye on the street, it wouldn't even cross my mind that the two of ye could be close in age. I wouldn't have a bar of it! No, I'd peg you for the younger woman; the glamorous second wife maybe."

Fiona watched as her mother began to thaw, a smile threatening to break through her pursed lips. She wasn't surprised—Ben had always been a charmer. Even when he was in secondary school, he'd had the young female teachers wrapped around his little finger. The guy could have been a top salesman if he'd applied himself—they all said it and had done for years.

Fiona might have called him out for waffling, but she was in no mood to see her mother in bad form. Instead, she changed the subject.

"What's the plan today, Ben?"

He shrugged. "Nothing much, now. I might call over to Billy and see what he's at."

"Is he not working?"

Ben shook his head. "No. He took holidays. They were meant to be going to Fuerteventura but then his girlfriend's leave got cancelled. Sickener. But it means he can play Playstation with me instead of floating around in a pool full of children's wee, so happy days for him I suppose."

Fiona baulked. Ben had never shown any desire to leave the country or to get a job, and she sometimes had trouble relating to the way he judged things offhand when he had never even bothered to try them out. "I'd say there's more to Fuerteventura than urine-filled swimming pools. Isn't there beaches? Walks you can do?"

He shrugged. "No idea. Never asked him. Sure why would you want to go to the beach?"

"Um, to swim in the ocean? To sunbathe?"

"If I wanted to sit around in water I'd have a bath. And isn't sunbathing dangerous?"

She rolled her eyes. "More dangerous than having six pints a night at Phelan's washed down by a kebab from the chipper?"

Her father cleared his throat. "Is that the pot calling the kettle black?"

"Dad!" she hissed. "You can't compare me having a few shots *one* night to Ben and his alcoholism! Sure he can't even describe himself as a functional alcoholic because he's too dysfunctional to get a job or a place of his own or—"

"Why would I get a place of my own?" Ben asked, looking wounded. "Mam and Dad love the company. And I'd only be throwing money away on rent. We're not all like you, getting the run of the pub and then driving it into the ground with your silly notions. You're not in Dublin now!"

Fiona rolled her eyes and dropped her fork, looking regretfully at the white pudding she hadn't yet had a chance to sample. "First of all, I'm paying rent. Dad'll tell you. Second of all, I'm quite happy to take criticism from anyone who's got the drive to go out there and work hard for themselves. I'm not prepared to take it from my unemployed twenty-six-year-old brother who's never worked an honest day in his life!"

"Fiona!" her mother gasped. "How can you say such a thing to him? Isn't he trying?"

"Trying? Is that what he's telling you?"

"Ah come on now. He finished school right when the economy was going down the toilet. What chance does he have? He's looking for work every day."

"He is in my eye. Unless Playstation is looking for testers."

"Quit it," Ben said, looking hurt.

Fiona sighed. "Sorry," she said. She meant it too—they had the kind of love-hate relationship that meant she struggled to hold back from tearing into him, but God help anyone who said a bad word about him in front of her. "I'm just worried about you. I don't like to see you wasting your life away when you could be doing something constructive."

"Like working in an office all day? Or studying for some useless degree that'll cost me thousands but won't get my foot in the door of a job?"

She winced. "There's no need to be so cynical. Why not give it a try and then judge how you like it?"

Her mother patted her arm. "Your sister has a point, love," she whispered. "It's not going to hurt you if you—"

"Jesus, Mary and Joseph!" Francis McCabe cried, so loud that all you could hear for a second afterwards was cutlery clattering onto the plates around him.

"What is it, Francis? Don't be yelling like that—you'll give me a heart attack so you will."

He looked up, red-faced. "Dec Hanlon. He's dead!"

Fiona rolled her eyes and leant down to massage her temples with her fingertips. "Ah for God's sake, Dad. What's he even done? Are those aul lads from Phelan's winding you up about him and me? I swear there's nothing going on and if there was it'd be none of your business."

She closed her eyes and wished she could be transported back to the pub. She was in no mood for a lecture about Dec so soon after the last one. She knew well that her father didn't like him, and it didn't matter: she had no interest in him as anything more than a friend.

For once, her mother stuck up for her. "She's right, Francis. Don't be giving her a hard time. She can see who she wants. And he's a good lad anyway. I don't know why you have such a bee in your bonnet about him. What did he ever do to you?"

Their father's silence made everyone look up. It wasn't like him to back down from an argument. He was sitting rigid, staring at the screen of his phone.

"What is it, Dad? You started it with your empty threats about him."

"Ah, Francis," Mrs McCabe weighed in. "What's the poor lad ever done to you?"

Finally, he looked up and stared her straight in the eye. Fiona couldn't read the emotion in his face but she was sure of one thing—it wasn't anger she was seeing. "I wasn't threatening him, Fi. I was reading this message from Finbarr."

"What are you on about?" she asked, half-laughing. She didn't like the look on her father's face. He seemed... uncomfortable about something. And why would her father's doctor friend talk about Dec? He lived in Newtownbeg and they only knew him because of their father. "Now Finbarr is threatening him?"

He shook his head and put his phone away. Then he reached up with both hands and wiped his face as if he was absolutely shattered after a long day's work. "No, love. Dec is dead. They found him down at the lock. They have to wait for the pathologist but someone called Finbarr when they couldn't get a hold of Dr Grimes. Finbarr reckons he's been dead since last night."

CHAPTER 6

Fiona unlocked the door that led up to the flat above the pub. Her parents had insisted that she was welcome to stay around, but she just wanted to be alone. Her mother was on the phone to anyone who would listen about how it was a terrible miscarriage of justice, while her father kept referring to Dec as if he was her tragic boyfriend.

She couldn't listen to it anymore. She wasn't a tragic widow, but he had been her friend. She just wanted to mull it over in peace. She ran up the stairs, growing lethargic before she'd even gotten to the top, and threw open the door that led to her little flat.

It wasn't much. When her father had run the pub, the rooms had been used as storage for extra crisps and other snacks from downstairs. There was no way their family of nine could have lived in the cramped flat. Those were different times— she remembered the pub being crammed with people every night of the week when she was a child in the nineties. It was different now in all the pubs. They were only really busy on special occasions.

When she had taken over the pub, she'd had to clear out boxes upon boxes of total clutter to even make a path through the mess. Who knew her parents were such hoarders? She had had no idea. Their house was kept immaculately clean and tidy. The flat above the pub was a different story. Buy and Sell magazines from the early nineties onwards, boxes of old glasses and other promotional rubbish from the breweries, an assortment of tools whose function she couldn't figure out. She had even found a stack of gundog guides from the eighties.

She threw herself on the couch and looked around. She had done a good job with the place with the help of her siblings and friends. Thinking about them made her think of Dec. She hadn't seen much of him in recent years, but he'd been around for most of her childhood.

And just like that, he was gone. She puffed out a breath of air as she recalled their conversation in the bar. He'd been down in the dumps, but that was understandable, wasn't it? He'd just gotten out of prison on a charge that most of the town didn't think was a legitimate reason to send someone to jail. Put that way, she was surprised he'd been doing as well as he was.

She closed her eyes and tried to remember every word of their conversations in the past few days. She wished she'd pushed him more to tell her how he felt. She had stopped herself, not wanting to seem nosy or pushy. Was there something he might have told her that could have helped her prevent…?

She shuddered and stood up quickly. She knew there was no sense in thinking like that but she couldn't stop dwelling on it.

She got a glass of water from the tiny kitchen and sat at the two-seater kitchen table instead. Soon she was drumming her nails on the surface, incapable of sitting still. It was as if all her senses were on high alert.

"Why am I so wired?" she muttered.

Sure, she'd had two lattes in quick succession that morning, but that was it. She'd had a huge breakfast that should have taken the edge off.

She sighed and closed her eyes before leaning back in her chair. The front legs came away from the floor and she carefully eased further and further back until her shoulders made contact with the wall behind. It was a movement she had to make carefully or risk sliding off and breaking her back.

"Breaking my back," she whispered. "Is that what happened to Dec?"

Her father's doctor friend hadn't been specific—or if he had, Francis McCabe had chosen not to share the details with his family.

And then she knew. Once she landed on it in her mind, she realised she had known it all along. After all, a thirty-year-old guy doesn't just die naturally, does he? Except it happened all the time. She sat forward, making a thud as the chair legs reconnected with the floor.

It was known to happen, but she was sure it hadn't in this case. And then she knew why.

"The guy with the glasses," she whispered, remembering. *So many people seemed so rattled by his presence… except for Dec. Why was that? Who is he?*

She reached for her phone and paused, realising what she was about to do was ridiculous. After all, she knew next to nothing about the case. The guards, on the other hand, would know everything there was to know. She sighed—not that she trusted the Gardaí of Ballycashel anymore.

She put the phone down and stood, brushing imaginary crumbs from her jeans.

She decided she would stop mulling over macabre theories and do something useful, like cleaning the floor in the pub downstairs before she got a visit from the health department. It would be just like Sergeant Brennan to set the bureaucrats on her and she'd be ready for them when they came with their clipboards and uptight expressions.

***

But the unsettled feeling wouldn't go away, no matter how hard Fiona scrubbed and cleaned and wiped. It took an hour of intense activity before she finally started to feel her anxiety begin to ebb away somewhat. So she was startled out of her wits when there was a loud banging on the door.

She was so numb it took her a few seconds to realise what it was. She jumped to her feet and tore off her pink rubber gloves with great difficulty.

"We're actually closed," she called as she hurriedly opened the first door. "We'll be open this evening."

She had decided to open that evening after all—to give her something to do, more than anything.

"Ah," she said, heart sinking. "Sergeant Brennan."

She'd been lucky, she supposed. He hadn't darkened her doorstep in a long time.

"Don't look so pleased to see me," he snapped in his efficient way.

"Don't worry," she muttered. "I won't."

Behind him, Garda Fitzpatrick cleared his throat. "Miss McCabe? We'd like to speak to you if you've got a moment."

She nodded and moved out of the way to let them in so she could lock up behind them. "Sure. Go on through, I'll just lock this back up."

"Worried about someone getting in?" the sergeant asked. "Have you had trouble lately?"

She rolled her eyes at his ram-rod straight back. "Of course not. No sense in leaving it open and having people wander in thinking we're open."

He turned and smirked back at her. "Chance'd be a fine thing, says you."

"I said no such thing. Things are going well here, Alex, you'll be pleased to know."

"It's Sergeant Brennan," he snapped.

She moved inside the bar. This was her domain, she reminded herself—he could throw his weight around all he wanted and it wouldn't change a thing. "Ah, I thought this was a social call seeing as you were so concerned about my business."

"Unfortunately not," he said with a tight smile. "We'd like to talk to you about Declan Hanlon."

She took a deep breath and told herself not to say anything that might stand against her. It was difficult, looking at his smug face across the bar, making himself comfortable in her place.

"What are those ciders like?" he asked, staring at the fridge behind her.

"Sorry," she said with a tight smile. "Till's closed."

He grunted.

"You wanted to ask me about Dec," she said.

"Yes. We've had a number of reports that the deceased was seen here in the hours leading up to his death."

She winced. "Can you not... never mind." There was little chance of humanity from Sergeant Brennan, whom she was sure was a card-carry sociopath. Her diagnosis was entirely unprofessional, having been made with reference to episodes of Dr. Phil and articles in the newspapers, but that didn't stop her from discussing it with her family, who all agreed wholeheartedly.

Alex Brennan looked affronted. He cleared his throat. "As I was saying, we're here to ask you about—"

"Dec," she said, holding up her hands. "Yes. He was here last night."

"Did you notice anything strange? Did he argue with anyone, for example?"

She shook her head. "No, not last night. He had a bit of a run-in with Gerry Reynolds the night before alright but—"

"So he was in here the night before as well?"

She nodded. "Yeah. First time I'd seen him since he got out." She chewed the inside of her cheek. Christ, she was angry—she couldn't even think about her friend without remembering why he'd found himself locked up in Mountjoy for three months. "Anyway. He kept himself to himself both nights, apart from…"

"Apart from?" Garda Fitzpatrick looked up from his notebook.

"There was a man. A stranger. Never seen him around here before. He came in and asked for a gin and tonic; got a bit shirty when I said we were all out of gin. Then he sat and chatted to Dec for ages. At first, I thought he was harassing the poor guy but there was no shouting; no aggression."

"What did they talk about?"

She shrugged. "I didn't hear."

Sergeant Brennan snorted. "What, don't tell me you had a rush of customers in!" He turned to Garda Fitzpatrick, whose laughter was as weak as it was forced.

"Very amusing, sergeant," she said, struggling not to roll her eyes. "Highly inappropriate given that you're here to investigate the murder of my friend."

He stopped writing and looked up at her. "Murder, you say. And how did you come to that conclusion? Did you fit a degree in forensic science somewhere in that illustrious career of yours?"

"Good God, Alex; you're even more bitter than I thought."

Garda Fitzpatrick sniggered but quickly changed it into a cough when his superior officer swung around and glared at him.

"I assume it's a murder. He's my age and he just got out of prison. Well, is it? Can you share or are you gonna sit there and simmer in self-importance for a little while longer?"

His eyes were narrowed to tiny slits. "You know I could arrest you for perverting the course of justice."

"I know it well," she said, leaning over the bar, so close to him that she could feel his astringent breath on her skin. "Didn't you do something similar to Dec and God knows he paid for it."

The sergeant went pale.

There, she thought. *Did it.*

She had told herself over and over that it wasn't worth getting into a verbal sparring match with Alex Brennan, but deciding that and trying to act on it were two different things entirely. She disliked him with every cell in her body and not just for what he'd done to Dec. But he was the Garda Sergeant in Ballycashel now, and like it or not, he held a lot of sway in the place.

She sighed. "Look, I just want to know what happened to my friend. Was he murdered? Can you at least tell me that?"

He wrinkled his nose. "I suppose. Yes. That's what we suspect, though we're waiting on the state pathologist. We think it's—"

She held up her hand. "Stop. I don't want to know the details." She closed her eyes and shook her head. "That's all I can think of. That man with the glasses and cap."

"And you'd never seen him around here before?"

She shook her head. "No."

"Do you think," the sergeant said, stroking his moustache. "That you could help one of my artists come up with a sketch?"

Fiona resisted the urge to point out that Sergeant Brennan didn't have an army of artists at his sole disposal. It wasn't the time. Nor would she have considered making the suggestion that she was about to make if it wasn't dire circumstances. But it was. She wanted them to find whoever did this to Dec, and she was willing to help in any way she could.

"I can do you one better," she said, pointing at a spot above the bar. "I can show you."

CHAPTER 7

"It's a bit grainy at times, but he was at the bar for ages," she said, rummaging in the cabinet under the TV for her laptop. "Hopefully you'll get a still you can use to identify him."

But Sergeant Brennan wasn't listening. Fiona pulled out the ancient laptop and stood to find him surveying her combined dining and living room with undisguised disdain.

"You actually live here, McCabe?"

"Yes," she said, refraining from making a crack about his rich father—just about. "Do you want to see the footage or not?"

His lips turned up in a smile that was gone a fraction of a second later. "Of course."

She took the seat beside Garda Fitzpatrick and turned on the laptop, trying not to flinch as she felt Sergeant Brennan move right behind her. Thankfully she had shut it down after she'd used it last so he wasn't able to see the fifty tabs of YouTube videos she usually saw when she flipped it open.

She opened a browser and logged into her camera software. The footage was saved for two weeks so there was no urgency in getting to it. She scanned through the list of filenames and clicked the one that covered the night before.

"Here we go," she said. "The camera is right above the bar, somewhat camouflaged by the menu board. To be honest I've never had to review the footage before, but it seemed high quality when we tested it after it was installed." She fell silent and watched. The time stamp said three in the afternoon. "Why don't I speed this up? It wasn't until later that your man came in."

"What time?"

She shrugged. The entire night was a blur to her now that something of such magnitude had happened. She wished she'd paid more attention, but how could she have known? "Maybe five? I'm not sure. It was busier than usual." She caught the smirk on his face. "Can we focus on Dec? You can get your digs in later. I'll even give you a deferred dig card if you'd like?"

"There's no need to be childish."

"You're..." she stopped and blew out a breath. "I can't remember what time. But I'll speed this up to eight times normal and then we'll see."

They sat in silence and watched as Dec entered and took a seat at the bar. Mrs Flannery shuffled in not long after and paid Dec no heed as she ordered a sherry and moved to a table at the back. Fiona slowed down the video to four times normal speed. The figures became slower and less jerky.

"Who was that who came in before Mr Hanlon?"

"Noel Cassidy," she said from memory. "And one of his friends."

The sergeant's eyes narrowed. "I hope you realise it's a serious crime to serve alcohol to minors."

Fiona sighed. "He's eighteen. And haven't you got bigger things to worry about?" She slowed the video to normal speed as someone zoomed in the door.

"There he is," she said, pointing at the stranger.

At this point, she and Dec had their heads bent together, deep in conversation. In the video, she didn't even look up. She stared at the screen aghast, wondering how she could have tuned out the sound of the bell.

Sergeant Brennan smacked his lips. "What's wrong with the sound?"

"No sound," she said, eye still glued to the screen.

"What's the point in that?"

She rolled her eyes. "That's a strange statement, Sergeant Brennan, when we're watching a video that might help you identify the killer." A shiver ran down her spine. "Who needs sound when you've got a visual? The cameras with proper sound were a little out of our price range. And to be honest, I only agreed to have this installed to keep my mam happy."

"Ah," he said, with a voice that sounded like it was dipped in vinegar. "The indomitable Mrs McCabe."

Fiona bristled. No one got to slag her mother, especially not Robocop. But she was too fascinated by what was happening on screen to call him up on it. Not that there was any point— her mother could take care of herself without Fiona rushing in on her white horse to save the day.

"There!" she said, tapping the screen.

Sergeant Brennan sucked in a breath. She could almost visualise him wincing. "You're not supposed to touch the screen."

"It's my laptop, Mr OCD. Would you look— this is it; the moment where he first makes contact with Dec."

"Makes contact," Sergeant Brennan mocked. "Someone's been spending too much time watching detective shows."

She rolled her eyes. "I'm sure that's where most of your detective experience has come from too, *Alexander*. What's the worst crime that happened in Ballycashel since you arrived? Johnny Baker's sheep breaking into Clancy's field? The kids at the primary school evading tax on the proceeds of their bake sale?" Her voice lowered. "Dec Hanlon not paying his TV licence?"

"Alright, calm down," Garda Fitzpatrick said quickly. "Let's just focus on this case without bickering."

"Fine," Fiona said, puffing out a breath. Why was she letting him get to her like this? She'd spent years despising him, but she'd managed to remain civil out of pure indifference. She told herself to get a grip.

"Are ye seeing this?" she asked after a few moments silence. "They're chatting away."

"Aye," Garda Fitzpatrick said with a nod. "Still no sign of your man's face."

Fiona gasped as the minutes ticked by in the corner of the screen. He was right. Everyone else who came into the bar looked up at the menu or the ceiling or *somewhere*. This guy, though, kept his head down the entire time.

"Do you think he was deliberately avoiding the cameras?" she asked, astonished. "Like he planned this whole thing out?"

It was becoming more and more likely. They'd been talking for several minutes and the guy still hadn't looked up. He managed to get off his stool and move out of view without once lifting his face. It looked even stranger when compared to the frequent glimpses they got of the other patron's faces.

Now, Dec glanced up at the menu and then looked away. A few more people entered the bar. Gerry came and sat beside Dec and they chatted for a while. Dec glanced back towards the toilet.

"I think we've seen all we need to see," Sergeant Brennan said.

But Fiona was transfixed. The man was back now, and there was something about Dec's demeanour that was different from before. "Look," she whispered, tapping the screen. "He's jerky now. Agitated."

He was indeed. His movements were more pronounced. He stretched his arms out and tapped them against the bar rail several times. Fiona frowned. To a stranger it might have looked like a weird little quirk, but she couldn't recall him ever doing something like that before.

"Did you see that?" she asked, not taking her eyes off the screen. "The way he's moving. It's—"

"Don't read into things," Sergeant Brennan snapped. "Why don't you speed it up a bit—I want to see if this gentleman's face makes an appearance. If not, I'd like you to work with one of my artists to come up with a sketch."

Fiona did as he asked and increased it to twice normal speed. The hen party came in, taking up most of the screen. They danced around the bar, for half an hour. The strange man left and Dec followed not long after him, as did Mrs Flannery.

"That's enough," Sergeant Brennan said.

Fiona shook her head in disbelief. "I had no idea. He seemed to be acting normally that night. Do you think he was deliberately avoiding the camera?"

Sergeant Brennan nodded. "That's what it looks like. I saw every other face that was in that bar, even the people who were sitting down the back."

She shuddered. "I think I can describe him. I'm not sure. Glasses. Grey hair and a cap. Around forty-odd."

"The artist will be able to get that out of you."

"Have you…" she hesitated. "Have you any other suspects?"

He smiled tightly. "I can't discuss the case with you at this point. We'll let ourselves out."

Fiona nodded and remained seated at the table. She stared at the frozen picture on the screen, with happy faces caught in various stages of laughter and merriment. She hadn't even noticed Dec leave, she'd been so busy with the crowd of customers.

She drummed her fingers on the table. Something was niggling her about the video. Was it just that glasses man had kept his head down? She tried to wipe it from her mind by watching YouTube videos, but she couldn't.

She got up to make a cup of tea and sat down in front of the laptop again. She moved the slider back close to the start of the video and started watching. Nothing else leapt out at her this time, but she almost spilt her tea when she watched Dec's strange stretch a second time.

He didn't just stretch out his arms and make that weird tapping motion, she saw now. He'd been fidgeting with a straw all night—she remembered noticing it at the time and the video had shown him reaching for it after he'd taken one of the matchbooks. Now she frowned as she noticed the straw appear on the bar in front of him, resting under his hand with about four inches exposed and pointing toward the spot where he had stretched his hands. Every so often, she could just about make out his thumb tapping on the black plastic.

Is he trying to tell me something? she wondered.

She dismissed that thought straight away. Of course he wasn't. He was messing around with a straw, she told herself. Fidgeting like most of the human population of Ireland did with click pens and straws and the like.

She shut off the laptop and moved to the couch to watch a movie. She chose the most gruesome thriller she could find on Netflix and settled in, hoping the fear would blot everything else from her mind.

But it didn't work. The same thought kept coming back to her over and over: Dec had never been a fidgeter. Never.

CHAPTER 8

With bleary eyes, Fiona ran down the back stairs that led to the pub. She had kept the pub closed and spent half the night in front of her laptop. When she wasn't watching the video, she was getting lost on google trails for hours as she searched for Morse code or other signals he might have been using. She could barely see straight now.

"Morning sis," Marty said as she unlocked the door for him. "I was afraid you weren't going to make it down at all. I need my coffee fix."

She grinned at him. He had never been a big coffee drinker and she knew he only stopped by every morning to support her—not that she'd ever let on that she knew.

"Sorry. The guards were over yesterday wanting to look at the camera footage from the bar. I spent half the night looking for something we might have missed."

"Oh right?" he said, looking serious as he took a stool at the bar and watched as she switched on the coffee machine. "What makes you think you missed something?"

She shrugged wearily. "I don't know. Just this feeling I got. Brennan doesn't care—all he cares is they seem to have got their man."

"Who is it?" Marty asked sharply.

She turned and appraised him. He was a gentle giant, but he had never been able to tolerate injustice against his friends and family. "They don't know yet," she said, a warning in her voice. "And when they find out I want to promise me you won't go after him. Leave it to the guards."

"What, Robocop and his fail army? Sure, that's the highway to justice right there."

"Marty! I don't want you getting in trouble over it! Anyway, the guy was smart enough to keep his face hidden. We didn't see one clear shot of it. I don't know who he is, but my money's on him being a hardened criminal." She shivered. "Maybe from one of those crime gangs you read about in the paper." She scratched her ear. "Though he didn't look like it. If I had to guess I would have said he was a schoolteacher."

"Maybe," Marty said, playing with a sachet of raw sugar. "He's a spy. All done up to look ordinary but secretly he works for the government."

"That's it!" Fi cried, gesturing excitedly at him.

"He's a spy?" Marty looked doubtful. "I'm not sure—it's a bit farfetched and probably down to the movie I watched last night."

"No, not that." She tapped his hand. "You messing with the sugar; it reminded me. Dec kept fidgeting. No, that's not right. He was calm for ages and then he started fidgeting. I've never known him to be a restless sort."

Marty shook his head. "Me neither. And I've known him since ye were both still in nappies. So you think the guy made him nervous?"

She sighed, not sure whether to voice her theory. On the one hand, it would be good to get a second opinion. On the other, she was too tired to handle the teasing Marty would no doubt give her if he thought her idea was crazy. Then a thought struck her. Who cared about her ego if it meant it helped find Dec's killer?

"Okay, so this is going to sound weird, right, but there was a part of the video where he suddenly lays out this straw he'd been messing with. And then he sort of." She paused and began to tap her index finger against the bar. "He started tapping it like this. And he was doing this big weird stretch like this." She copied the movement and then waited silently for Marty's opinion.

"So what do you think it was?"

She shook her head. "I thought it might be some kind of code; like Morse code? But I don't know. I tried to jot down whether they were long or short taps but they all looked the same to me. And there was no rhythm to it. I don't know—I feel like it's some kind of code if only I could decipher it."

"Fiona," Marty said seriously. "I don't mean to knock your theory or anything, but think about it for a second. This is Dec we're talking about. He was a great fella and a hard worker, but you're saying he whipped out a complicated code just like that? I don't know…"

She felt like the wind had been let out of her sails. He was right and she knew it. "What then?" she asked desperately.

"I don't know," he said with a shrug. He must have seen the defeat in her face because he stood up all of a sudden. "Let me have a look at this video. Where's your laptop?"

***

Fiona looked up hopefully when the door at the back of the pub opened. "Well?"

He shook his head. "I don't know. He was up to something alright, but I can't for the life of me figure out what it is."

She sighed. "Fair enough. Thanks for looking. Here I'll make you a fresh coffee—this one's getting cold."

He said nothing. She thought nothing of it until she turned around and saw he had vanished.

"Marty?" she asked. It wasn't like him to just disappear without saying goodbye: everyone in her family was notorious for not being able to leave a room without saying it at least five times. Besides, she would have heard the bell in the otherwise empty bar.

There was a grunting sound from close by. Alarmed, she hoisted herself up and leant over the bar. Sure enough, he was off his chair and on the ground.

"Marty!" she cried, jumping down again and running around behind him. "What happened? Are you hurt?"

He muttered something and she was on her feet again in an instant, reaching across the bar for her phone.

"Mam! It's me!" she shrieked about a second after hitting 2 and speed dialling home. She could always rely on her mother to pick up before the third ring. Even if she was busy, Mrs McCabe had such an insatiable appetite for gossip that she kept the portable phone near her at all times— even when she was gardening or having a bath. "It's Marty. Oh, you better send Dad over. I'll call an ambulance now. He's taken a fall and I can't get any sense out of him and—"

She gasped as the phone was pulled away from her. She spun around in shock.

"Mam, I'm fine," Marty said. "No, I'm fine. Really. No, I'm not just having you on. I was busy looking at something under the bar and she mistook it for me being injured." He paused and Fiona could hear the faint buzz of her mother's voice. "No, it's not mice. Just some… look, don't worry about it. Okay, I'll be there. Bye, bye bye. Bye. Okay, bye."

Fiona rolled her eyes. "When you didn't answer I thought something was up with you— like you'd had a stroke or something."

He shook his head, eyes gleaming. "Not at all. No, I started thinking about that video. I knew Dec had to be up to something."

It was the excited look in his eyes that made her realise he had solved the puzzle. Sure enough, he held up a little piece of cardboard. Fiona's heart plummeted.

"Ah," she said, shaking her head. "I don't know what I expected. That's just one of the matchbooks I had printed up for this place. Remember? You all thought they were hilarious."

But Marty looked no less pleased with himself. "I know that." He flipped open the little book. "Look at this, Fiona. I think you were on to something."

She leant forward and a shiver ran down her spine at the sight of the spindly words on the side opposite the little row of skinny matches.

"Oh God," she gasped.

Marty nodded grimly. "Do you recognise the writing? Is it his?"

She nodded. They may have only gone out for a few weeks, but it was in that early teenage stage where it was practically mandatory to write each other long and soppy notes on pages torn from the middle of school copybooks. She'd have recognised that distinctive spidery writing anywhere.

"It's Dec's alright," she said, shaking her head. "But this means…" she stopped and shivered again, trying to make sense of it. "This means something was going on alright. It wasn't spontaneous—he knew he was in trouble."

She took the book from Marty and stared at the writing in blue pen. *Danger. HQ. Dash*, it said, with the last word underlined.

"See here," she said, pointing below the writing. "It's a faint pen line like he was about to write more and got disturbed."

He nodded. "You're right."

"Probably Gerry," she said, remembering how Dec hadn't been alone for long. "It doesn't make sense—why didn't he just say something to me? This makes no sense."

"Maybe he was afraid?"

She shook her head. "Maybe, but he seemed calm as anything."

"He could have been keeping a brave face on it—not wanting to have anything kick off in the bar. Or he might not have realised the severity of what he was involved in."

They fell silent, both staring at the text on the cardboard. Fiona held it up to the light on the off chance that there was something else on there.

"I don't understand it," she said after several moments' silence.

"Me neither," Marty said. "It's not like Dec to be so vague. Not even vague... this makes no sense."

"Was there anything else down there?" she asked hopefully.

"Nothing," Marty said, shaking his head. "I found it wedged into a knot under the bar. There's nothing else down there apart from a few blobs of chewing gum."

Fiona winced and was about to comment but thought better of it. After all, other peoples' bad habits kind of paled in comparison to what had happened to Dec. "I'll freeze it off later. What do you think I should do with this?"

Marty shrugged and took the matchbook back again, before dropping it on the bar. "Fingerprints," he explained, reaching for a paper napkin. "We should probably get this to the guards. That's all we can do. I'll drop it over to the station now if you want."

Fiona sighed. "You're right. Here, let me get a picture of that before you do. Just in case we think of something."

He was holding it up for her to photograph when the door of the bar burst open. Fiona looked at Marty in alarm—she was sure she'd locked both doors when she let him in.

CHAPTER 9

Marty lifted his stool and held it forward as if he was going to use it to defend them both. It would have looked ridiculous if anyone else had done it, but his sheer power and height made him look extremely intimidating. By the time the inner door opened, Fiona almost felt comfortable that everything was going to be fine no matter who had come for them. The only logical conclusion she could draw was that it was the strange man with the glasses—he had somehow found out that they had footage of him.

It soon became obvious that her imagination was running rampant.

"What are you doing here, Mam? I thought you were someone breaking in."

Mrs McCabe turned to her with a furious look that Fiona knew all too well. "You frightened the life out of me, calling me up and telling me something was wrong with Marty. Sure I had to come down here and see with my own eyes that he was alright." She stared at her oldest son, still frozen with the stool held up like he was about to attack her. "And here I see he's acting the gurrier. What, would you hit your own mother with that thing?"

He sighed and dropped the stool. "No, Ma. We didn't know it was you, see. After all the..." he stopped and glanced at Fi. She shot him a warning look back.

Unfortunately, their mother picked up on the silent message that went between them.

"What are ye two up to?" Mrs McCabe demanded in the dangerously low voice that meant she thought she was onto something. She was like a beagle once she picked up the scent of something amiss—there was little anyone could do to throw her off the trail.

"Nothing," they both said in unison.

But it was too late—Mrs McCabe had sensed something was going on and they knew she wouldn't rest—or leave—until she got to the bottom of it. Her attention shifted from her children to the piece of card that was still in Marty's hand.

"What's that?"

He stared back at her helplessly.

"It's one of my matchbooks," Fiona said quickly. "Marty's helping me with some marketing."

Her mother's eyes narrowed. "Marty is?" she repeated, her voice dripping with scepticism. "My son Marty, who thought it was a good idea to put up a billboard on the Dublin Road with that awful poster of the girls in bikinis. How did you think that was going to advertise the hardware shop?"

Fiona couldn't help but smirk. Her brother turned the colour of beetroot. "You have to admit it was a good idea. Gung-ho marketing. He's a guru, see?"

Her mother wasn't buying it. Fiona wasn't surprised—you didn't do things like that in a town like Ballycashel. To make matters worse, Father Jimmy had been mortally offended and had chosen to highlight the issue during Sunday mass. Mr and Mrs McCabe had decamped to Newtownbeg for mass for several months after that, unable to bring themselves to show their faces in Ballycashel church.

"You're lying to me," her mother snapped. "I can tell. That weird thing happens with your lip."

Fiona closed her eyes and gasped. "Your words—they cut like a knife."

"Stop changing the subject, Fiona McCabe. I'm not leaving here until you tell me what's going on."

"We're just taking some pictures to put on my website."

Her mother crossed her arms; there was no way on earth she believed this. "Why didn't you ask Enda to help with that big fancy camera of his?"

"He's in Lourdes. And my phone's just as good."

"Nonsense," Mrs McCabe fired back. "Especially not in here with this light. You'd need a big proper setup with lights and the like."

"And how exactly would you know this?" Fiona demanded, forgetting about the investigation for a moment.

Her mother looked affronted. "I watched a programme on YouTube about it. Beginner photography it was called." She sniffed. "It's a shame the pair of ye didn't watch it; you might have thought up a better lie."

Fiona's stomach rumbled and she rolled her eyes. She knew well from past experience that this could and would stretch on for hours. "Fine," she said. "If you must know, the guards were over last night looking at the footage from the cameras here. They reckon the suspect is a guy that was in here talking to Dec on the night he was killed."

Mrs McCabe flushed. "A murderer!" she cried. "Here in our bar! Oh, Fiona. It's not safe."

"But you worked here for years when Dad had the pub! I don't know what you're on about."

"Those were different times," her mother said primly.

"You're telling me that murder was only invented in the years since you and Dad stopped running the pub?"

"Don't be difficult. No, I'm telling you that it's not something that happened in a little place like Ballycashel. I don't know." She shook her head as if to emphasise her disbelief. "Is it the internet or the motorways? The world's been turned on its head." She sat down at the bar. "Right. So what have we got?"

Fiona glanced at Marty, who shrugged helplessly. "Sure we might as well tell her if we're bringing it to the guards anyway. They're as useless as a brown paper bucket."

"Fair point. Okay Mam, we didn't see much on the video but Dec was acting weird. Marty found this matchbook shoved up under the bar where he was sitting. Here, have a look. Just don't touch it in case they need to fingerprint it."

Mrs McCabe retrieved her glasses from the cord around her neck and carefully opened the matchbook with the napkin Fiona slid across the bar to her.

"It's his writing alright," she said conclusively.

"How'd you know?"

"Because I remember it well from having to fish his notes out of the pockets of your school skirt."

Fiona flushed.

"You should've been more careful at hiding your things," her mother said. "At least he could spell—not like that Tony fella you went out with him after."

"Tony Fisher?" Marty repeated with undisguised disgust. "Please tell me you didn't."

Fi shrugged, unable to look either of them in the eye. What was it about close family that had the ability to reduce you to a moody teenager? she wondered. "We went out for about a week. I'm not sure we even held hands before he dumped me for Susan Cassidy. They're still together now."

"Lord bless us and save us," her mother said, shaking her head. "You'd a lucky escape there, Fiona."

Fiona was amazed—she hadn't been in touch with Tony since then, but he must have been bad news if her mother wasn't actively trying to set her up with him. Still, she had no desire to open up that can of worms.

"What do you think it means?"

Their mother shook her head. "Danger. HQ. Dash," she read. "It doesn't make sense."

"I know," Fiona said. "It's some kind of cry for help—we can all agree on that, but I have no clue apart from that. Not that we need to decipher it—I've told the guards about the man he was with and even though there's no clear picture of him, they think I might be able to help by working with an artist to do a photofit of him."

"And who was there when Declan wrote this?"

Fiona shrugged. "Loads of people. Noel Cassidy. Mrs Flannery. Will Connolly. Gerry Reynolds. Mary and Pete Prendergast... No, wait. The Prendergasts left before Dec could have hidden the—"

"Gerry Reynolds," her mother said thoughtfully. "And I was never a big fan of that Prendergast."

"That's been well documented through the years."

"Less of your sarcasm," Mrs McCabe huffed. "Sure I'm only trying to help."

"There's not much point, Mam. It all seems to point to this guy. Gerry and Dec had a few words the night before in the pub, but show me one person in this town who hasn't had a run-in with Gerry Reynolds."

"He's no good."

"I know that. But he's clever about it, unfortunately. They've never been able to pin anything on him. Anyway, the guards are convinced it's this fella with the glasses."

"Where's he from? Let me have a look at him. Sure how do they even know it was him and not Gerry?"

"No, Mam, come on. I've got things to do here."

"Sure I'll just go look at it and you can be getting on with your work down here."

Not likely, Fiona thought. *You'll have a good look at my search history and sign me up to God knows what dating sites while you're at it.* "I'll bring the laptop over tonight. You can look at it then."

"You're trying to fob me off."

"I am not!" Fiona cried. "I didn't open at all last night and if I'm to open this evening I need to get started now. You can stay and give me a hand if you like."

"Sure didn't I spend years raising you and I still make you lovely dinners. What more do you want from me?"

"What if she's right?" Marty said, as the door closed behind their mother and she locked up after herself with the keys that she was only meant to use in emergencies.

"What do you mean?" Fiona asked absently as she started chopping lemons.

"Well, what if it's not this guy in the video?"

Fiona stopped. The guards had been so convinced that there was only one suspect and she hadn't seen fit to question that. What did she know about investigations? And she believed them too, on this occasion. She shrugged. "It makes sense, doesn't it? This guy shows up in town and then a few hours later Dec is dead. If it was someone local, then why wouldn't they have killed him before now? He's been home for weeks, you said. The timing is just too suspicious."

"Yeah," Marty said, nursing his now-cold coffee. "You know there's something familiar about him too."

Excitement and dread shot through Fiona in equal measure. "You mean you spotted his face in the video? This is massive! We've got to tell someone."

"No," he said, shaking his head slowly. "It was more to do with his... I don't know—his presence?"

Fiona gasped. "You mean he might be from one of those crime gangs? Like a crime boss?" She immediately froze in horror. "A gangster in my bar. My God, Marty; and I was short with him too. What if he comes back for me?"

Marty's smile was long gone. He stood, alert and imposing. "He won't get near you."

"He will if he's a crime lord, Marty. They're devious. He could be in here right now and we wouldn't even know. Didn't I tell you he just appeared in here? I thought I'd been distracted but what if some of his henchmen disabled the bell?"

"Right," he said decisively. "That's it. We're going to that Garda station and we're not leaving until they have that artist come and draw his picture. Then I'm sure they can run his picture through their systems and whatnot."

"But what about the bar? And the shop?"

"They can wait. Your safety is more important." He crossed his arms and stared her down. "Come on. We'll go now."

Marty McCabe was in full-on protective big brother mode, and for once Fiona didn't object.

CHAPTER 10

Sergeant Brennan stared across his neat desk at them as if they were solely responsible for interrupting the police activities of all of Ireland.

"I've put in a call to my superiors and requested an artist. I haven't heard back yet."

Marty sat back in his chair and crossed one long leg over the other knee. The sergeant was intimidated by him and he used it to his best advantage. "Sure what else are you doing? There's not another murder investigation going on in town that no one's aware of, is there?"

Sergeant Brennan smiled a tight-lipped grimace. "Luckily there's not, Mr McCabe. I don't know how you can joke about such a thing."

Marty sat forward. "And I don't know how you can sit there and act so unconcerned. There's a murderer on the loose and he was in my sister's pub on the night of the murder. She could be in danger."

Fiona shivered. Was it true? Was it possible that he'd come after her? It wasn't like she'd seen anything… she froze. Of course, she'd seen his face, hadn't she? She could identify him.

"Has anyone else mentioned him to ye in the course of your investigation?"

Sergeant Brennan shook his head. "A few people talked about seeing Dec at the bar, but no one mentioned his companion. I'm afraid you're our only lead here."

Fiona gripped her chair. "So I'm the only one who can identify this guy," she said faintly. "Meaning he could come after me to make sure you never get your photofit."

"This isn't a film," Sergeant Brennan sneered. "Nor is it inner city Dublin."

"Oh yeah?" Fiona said, rankled. "Well my friend was murdered a few days ago. So things around here aren't as happy clappy as you make out."

"Miss McCabe—"

"What we're saying is," Marty interrupted smoothly. "We've expressed our concern for my sister's safety. Now if anything was to happen to her, I'd naturally see to it that all the newspapers were made aware of your indifference to the threat against her life."

"Mr Mc—"

Marty continued as if the sergeant hadn't spoken. "And I don't think there's any amount of political clout that'll get you off the hook for such negligence. You'll be stuck holding a speed camera until you can collect your pension."

By now, Sergeant Brennan was red with frustration and sullenly silent. "I have other cases," he said finally.

"Oh yeah, like what?" Fiona probed. "Clancy's missing gate? Who drew the graffiti on the old schoolhouse?"

"It's confidential Garda business."

"Career suicide if anything happens to my sister," Marty said, as casually as if he was commenting on the latest results from the Premier League.

***

Marty's words had the desired effect. Within two hours, they were ushered into a small interview room and joined by a man with laptop and drawing tablet. Fiona closed her eyes and described the man's features as accurately as she could. She was dismayed to see that the artist's impression looked nothing like the man she had seen in the pub.

Little by little, however, he made changes and a resemblance began to form. It took two hours before she sat back and nodded decisively.

"That's him," she said to Marty as much as to the Garda artist. "That's the guy who was in the pub that night. It's exactly like him down to the hateful smirk."

***

They returned to the pub, intending to open. Mrs McCabe had clearly had other ideas.

"I don't believe this," Fiona said, as she tried to turn her key in the lock for the third time.

She knew there was no point, but she could scarcely believe that her parents had had the gall to do it. The shiny new brass lock told her all she needed to know.

"Are they serious?"

Marty shook his head solemnly. "They must have gone to the shop while we were at the Garda station. I've got ones just like this in stock. I hope they left money for it—they're expensive yokes."

"Hardly the point, Mart." She smiled as she thought of something. "But they can't have locked me out of my own home—even our parents wouldn't be that mad."

She abandoned the pub door and walked around the side of the building to the entrance that led directly upstairs to the flat. For a moment she was apprehensive, but then she saw with relief that the lock was as dull and tarnished as it had always been. She smiled back at Marty and disappeared upstairs.

The flat seemed untouched. She hurried through, calling back to Marty. "They're not as clever as they thought they were."

The smile soon vanished from her face. The door to the pub was closed as usual, but there was a sign hanging from it that hadn't been there that morning.

"What is it?" Marty asked, coming up behind her.

Fiona read it through gritted teeth.

We're not going to sit by and let you put yourself in harm's way alone at night.

"What the hell?" she hissed.

"They have a point," Marty said, sounding reluctant.

"But you said you'd stick around," she cried. "I'd already decided to reduce my opening hours until they catch the guy."

She tried the door knowing it was futile. There was a shiny new lock on that door too.

"I know, but I suppose it's safer this way." Marty wouldn't look her in the eye as he said it.

***

If she was expecting any contrition from her parents, she was disappointed. For starters, it was her father who answered the phone—he never usually got near the thing in time to answer it.

"Oh it's you," he said, sounding almost sullen.

"Yeah it's me," she snapped. "You know, the tenant of your pub who you've illegally locked out of the premises. I should call the guards."

"We did it for your own good. There's a murderer out there."

"And what about my bank balance, ha? That'll be murdered too if you force me to keep the pub closed."

"That's in poor taste, Fiona McCabe," her father shot back.

She rolled her eyes. This was coming from a man who makes tasteless jokes at expense of most people in the town. "So is changing the locks. You can't do that! I pay rent!"

"You need to cop on."

Fiona groaned and threw her head back. "I need to cop on? I'm twenty-nine years old. This is my business; my livelihood. You can't just lock the doors and keep me out."

"No? Well that's what I've done. And I'm not giving you the keys until this whole affair is straightened out."

"But that could be weeks," she groaned. "You know what the guards are like here."

"So be it," he said simply. "I'll give you a rebate of your rent to cover the time you're closed. You can't get fairer than that."

She groaned. "I don't want a handout! I want to be able to run my business as normal like any other business person."

She heard a click and knew immediately that it was her mother on the other phone. "You wouldn't be able to run your business from the grave, now would you?" she said testily.

Fiona's hand shot up to her temple to massage away the beginning of a tension headache. "That's a stupid thing to say. Obviously I wouldn't, but I'm not going to die."

"You don't know that. You said yourself that this guy could be dangerous."

Fiona flipped around to face her brother and narrowed her eyes. "I don't remember saying that to you, Mam."

Marty wouldn't meet her eyes. For a big guy, he looked pretty awkward at that moment. Fiona sighed. She finally realised she wasn't going to get anywhere with them on this. "Fine," she muttered. "I'm not happy about this, though," she said before hanging up.

***

"Have ye found him yet?"

Sergeant Brennan groaned on the other end of the line. "Not in the half an hour since you last called, no."

Fiona stared at the clock above the kitchen table in dismay. Had it really only been half an hour? Despite her family's protests, she had insisted on staying in the flat that night. She saw their reasoning but nothing could have made her spend the night in the family home, not after they'd infantilised her to the extent that they'd changed the locks on her own pub so she couldn't open up.

It was turning out to be a long evening, though.

"Nothing?" she asked, despairing. "You must have run him through your systems by now."

Sergeant Brennan laughed. "Have you actually seen our systems?" he asked, in the most cordial tone he'd addressed her with since she'd met him.

"No of course not," she snapped. "I'm not a guard or a computer hacker or whoever else has access to your systems."

"Well," he said, sounding noticeably cooler now. "They're not that advanced. I did assure you that we'd be in contact when there's a development in the case."

Fiona managed to stop herself from responding that his word was as good to her as a hole in the head. She needed him at the moment and didn't want to cause even more bad blood between them.

"I want to know the minute you get him."

"It doesn't work like that," he said with a pained sigh. "Look, I need to go. The taxpayers aren't paying me to sit here and coddle you."

"Fine," she said quickly. "I'll call you in an hour to see if there's an update." She hung up before he could respond.

CHAPTER 11

By eight o'clock, Fiona was going out of her mind. There was nothing on TV and none of her friends or siblings were answering their phones, probably at the behest of her mother. It was just like Mrs McCabe to intimate those around her into silence so she had no choice but to return to the family home to alleviate her boredom.

The problem was, every show that Fiona landed on invariably had something to do with crime or criminals and she was already far more frightened than she'd let on to anyone. It was only indignation at her parent's actions and her extreme stubbornness that stopped her from running to her parents' house like a baby.

Why wouldn't she be scared, she thought as she looked around the room scanning the nooks and crannies under the furniture for lurking hitmen. But she wouldn't give her family the satisfaction of telling them. They had babied her for too long—she was going to show them by standing on her own two feet—even if in order to do that she had to down an entire bottle of Jameson and get legless in the process.

She sighed and checked the clock. It was five past eight, a whole thirty minutes since she'd last called Sergeant Brennan. Far too long, she decided, pulling the phone closer.

The phone rang for so long that she thought he must be screening her calls. Finally he answered just as she was contemplating ending the call and dialling again.

"Sergeant Brennan," he said in his efficient way.

"Any word?" Throughout the course of the evening, she had gradually stopped introducing herself and started getting straight to the point.

"Fiona," he said, sounding like a long-suffering teacher. "It's you."

"It is," she said impatiently. "And you're you. Now, can you tell me what's going on? Have ye got him?"

Her finger hovered over the end call button, so convinced was she that he'd tell her there was no news and that she should leave him alone.

This time, however, he didn't say anything of the kind.

"I can't discuss the details of an—"

"You do!" she cried, relieved beyond words. "If you didn't, you would have told me to stop calling just like you did the last few times."

"It wasn't a few times," he said coldly. "It was more like twenty. I should charge you with wasting Garda time."

Fiona rolled her eyes. "Sure you're probably sitting there with your feet up watching cat videos…" she squeezed her eyes closed—she could have kicked herself. She figured that was exactly what he was doing, but she needed him right now. "Oh, and highly important Garda business, of course. Now, what's the latest?"

"You're all charm, Miss McCabe. But I can't—"

She shifted in her chair. Against all odds, she found she was enjoying this conversation with Robocop—maybe it was down to the fact that there had been a development in the case. "Well, if you won't tell me over the phone, how about I come down to the station and you can tell me in person?"

Her threat had the desired effect. He sighed long and low. "That won't be necessary, I assure you."

"Well tell me so, otherwise I'll have no choice."

"Fine," he snapped. "But you'd better not breathe a word about this to anyone."

"I won't."

"We've had several reports on our tipline. People convinced they've seen a man identical to the one in the photofit image."

"You've got him then?"

He cleared his throat. "Not a word to anyone, Miss McCabe. Yes, it appears that way. A unit has been sent to an abode in south Dublin."

***

"You may give me those new keys," Fiona said by way of greeting as she let herself into her family home.

Ben looked up. "I didn't expect to see you here this evening—thought you'd be sulking in the flat over some rom-com."

She pulled a face at him. Even Ben's jibing wouldn't ruin her good mood. "You were in on it as well? That's great—nice to know you were all keen to gang up on me. I'll remember that when I'm rolling in money and you come to me asking for a loan."

He shrugged. "I had no choice—Dad made me come and help him. I didn't exactly want to."

"That's because you don't want to do *anything*," she reasoned. "Where are they anyway?" By now she had seen that her parents weren't in the room like she'd expected.

"In the sitting room watching the news."

Fiona pulled out her phone and stared at the blank screen. She had made Sergeant Brennan promise to tell her when the suspect had been successfully captured, but there was still no word from him. It would have been all the sweeter to have the matter stitched up before she announced it to her parents and demanded the keys back, but she'd take whatever wins she could get.

She rushed to the sitting room and threw open the door.

"They have the murderer," she announced.

"We're watching something," her mother said sullenly.

"They have him," Fiona repeated. "Brennan told me. Give me back the keys."

With a pained expression, her father jabbed violently at the remote control and the noise stopped abruptly.

"Can I not get a moment's peace in my own home?" he said, sounding very put-upon.

"Sure you can," Fiona said brightly. "Just hand over the keys and you can have all the peace you want. Oodles of it, in fact."

"We did it for your own good," her mother said, looking outraged.

"I don't care about that anymore," Fiona said. "All I care about is that this is over and I can go back to running my business. I appreciate your concern, though I wish you hadn't been so heavy-handed about it."

"We're to take your word for it, are we?" her father said, reaching for the remote again.

"Well, yeah," she said, frowning. "I'm not going to lie to you about something like this."

"Are you not?" he asked, his eyes boring into hers. "It seems like exactly the kind of thing you might do, say if it was the only way you could get the keys back. Why don't you just relax and read a book or something?"

"I don't want to relax," she huffed. "I've been closed for two days as it is—I need to get in there and prep for tomorrow. If I don't open I'll have to throw out a load of fresh ingredients. It's a total waste of money. I can't believe I'm having to explain this to you."

"Your safety is more important than the bar."

"Fine," Fiona said. "If you won't believe me, you can hear it for yourself from the horse's mouth. I'm calling Robocop."

"Ah God," her father said, throwing up his arms. "The last thing I want to do of an evening is talk to that bollix."

"Sorry, but it's the only way I'm going to get you to believe me." She pulled out her phone and tapped the number at the top of her call log.

"Sergeant Brennan."

"It's me, Fiona McCabe. You're on speaker. I'm here with my parents."

Brennan groaned faintly. "Lovely. To what do I owe the honour?"

"No one likes a smarty pants," Mrs McCabe muttered.

"I heard that," Sergeant Brennan said.

"Good," she shot back. "I wanted you to. Fiona tells us you've caught your man who killed poor Declan."

Sergeant Brennan groaned. "I thought I asked you to keep that between ourselves, Miss McCabe."

Fiona shrugged, supremely unconcerned. "Well it was a matter of importance for my business. Anyway, can you tell them? You must have got him, right? It was over an hour ago when your SWAT team was outside his house."

"SWAT team," Mrs McCabe gasped.

"It wasn't a SWAT team," Sergeant Brennan said. Fiona could almost picture the sour expression on his face as he said it. "And yes, actually, they were successful in locating the person of interest."

"See?" Fiona said, looking at her parents triumphantly. "They got him."

She hung up, hoping she'd never have to call Sergeant Brennan again.

CHAPTER 12

"Do you want some food or are you still sore at us for trying to save your life?" Mrs McCabe called, bustling into the dining room with a tea towel over her shoulder.

Fiona shook her head and laughed. "Only you two could make a joke out of denying me all of my rights as a tenant. Remind me again why I shouldn't have called the guards?"

"Because Robocop can't stand the sight of you and he wouldn't have come to your rescue even if you offered him a million euro?" Kate offered.

"There is that, I suppose," Fiona conceded. "Still, though. You can't be doing that. Promise me now—you'll never pull any funny business like that. I'm renting the pub and I paid for all of the refurbishments. And it turned out your man had gone back to Dublin so there was no need to worry about him lurking around in Ballycashel."

"We weren't to know that," her father said from behind his paper.

"That's not the point," Fiona said. Her heart wasn't in the argument—it was all over now so she didn't see any reason to dwell. Aside from the obvious desire to make sure they never pulled a funny one like that again. Even then, Fiona didn't see how they could—it wasn't like murder was a regular occurrence in Ballycashel.

"What is it with you and Robocop anyway?" Ben asked. "I mean, I know he's a pain and all, but he seems like one of those jumped up corporate fellas who're trying to get up the ladder. Why would he have it in for a no-hoper like you?"

Fiona winced. "Ouch! Less of the no-hoper business if you don't mind. Especially coming from you."

"What?" Ben protested. "I'm working. Well, working on working."

"You're not exactly Richard Branson."

"Neither are you."

She shrugged. "Don't want to be. I'd settle for running a successful pub thank you very much."

"She's trying to change the subject," her mother announced, before leaning in as if she was about to share a fascinating conspiracy with them all. "The reason Fiona and Sergeant Brennan are at each other's throats, I believe, is because of a lingering attraction to each other."

"Ah jaysus," Ben said, cringing and covering his face as if he'd just been told the intimate details.

"Mam!" Fiona protested. "There is no such thing. I can't stand the man."

"That's what people always say when they're really in love. It's the attraction between you, see? The chemistry."

"Ugh," Fiona said, staring in dismay at her food, which no longer seemed so appetising. "You've been watching too many sappy films. Sometimes when two people are at each other's throats it's just a sign that they can't stand each other. Is that too hard to believe?"

"Well, yeah," Ben said slowly, as if he was reluctant to get involved less he hear something gruesome he couldn't get out of his mind. "You do seem to hate the guy."

"So does Dad," Fiona pointed out. "That doesn't mean Dad's about to run off and become Mr Brennan."

"Too right!" Francis McCabe bellowed. "I can't stand the man either. Even looking at his little pea-head makes me start to lose my temper."

"All part of the chemistry," Fiona smiled, enjoying the rage that emanated from her father. He was still hidden behind his paper of course, but it didn't matter—she could tell from his white-blue knuckles that he was getting madder and madder by the second.

Then Francis surprised them all. He put his paper down and folded it in that precise way of his. "I believe Fiona is trying to distract us all from the fact that she's known Sergeant Brennan far longer than the rest of us. They were first acquainted in Coppers, I believe."

Fiona glared across the table at her sister, who had the good sense to pretend to be focused on her phone. "What would you know about Coppers?" she asked her father. "Back when you lived in Dublin it was all trad bands and the like. Coppers hadn't even been invented then."

"You think ye young ones invented having the craic? Sure I heard all about Coppers when I was training the minor hurlers. And to think my own daughter was in there, gallivanting with that Robocop fella. It brings shame to the family, Fiona."

Fiona's cheeks burned. Her 'thing' with Sergeant Brennan couldn't even be called a thing, but he was so reviled in her household that she could scarcely bear to think about it. "I can't believe you told them, *Catherine*."

Kate looked astonished. "Of course I told them. It was hilarious. I can't imagine you with that fella. My skin crawls even looking at him, never mind talking to him... or whatever else."

Fiona shuddered. "There was none of that."

"Eeeugh," her father and brothers groaned in unison.

"For the love of God," Francis McCabe said with a heavy sigh. "We don't want to hear the gruesome details."

"You were the one who brought it up!"

"Well your brother wanted to know why there's such animosity between the two of you. He certainly didn't ask for a blow-by-blow account of your relationship. No one should have to hear that."

Fiona felt like dropping her head into her bowl she was so exhausted by their barrage of questions. "It wasn't a relationship." Realising there was no way she could change the subject without them changing it back, she resigned herself to telling them the whole story—if only to satisfy their curiosity and shut them up. "Okay fine. By the way, Kate, I'm never telling you anything again."

"Fine by me," Kate said with a supremely disinterested shrug. "It's not like you do anything interesting these days anyway."

Fiona ignored her. "Okay, I met him in Coppers one night. As you do."

"What in God's name," her mother interrupted as she sat down. "Is Coppers?"

"It's a nightclub in Dublin," Marty offered immediately. "Where people go to shift guards."

Fiona ran her fingers through her hair and beseeched herself to remain calm.

"You went out one night with the sole purpose of shifting guards?" Mrs McCabe said incredulously.

"Please, Mam," Ben said, looking pained. "Can you not say that word? It's creeping me out hearing it from you."

Mrs McCabe looked mortally insulted. "What, you think just because I'm your mother that I'm not capable of having a passionate side too? I'm sure there were places we went when we wanted to shift guards too."

"Ah, Mam," Kate howled. "Please stop. You'll make me vomit. Sure there were no guards around in your time. Weren't they established after the civil war?"

Everyone around the table fell silent. Fiona sent a silent thanks in her sister's direction, not sure whether to completely forgive her for being the one to bring up the subject in the first place.

"Excuse me," Mrs McCabe said in the low voice that she reserved for when she was well and truly affronted. "Exactly how old do you think I am?"

Kate managed to keep her face calm—Fiona had no idea how she managed it. The others' faces reflected a mixture of amusement and sheer disbelief. Francis McCabe had wisely chosen to return his attention to his newspaper.

"I don't know," Kate whispered. "I'm not up on the history myself. Wasn't it around nineteen twenty five they formed the Free State?"

"Catherine McCabe!"

"Oh," Kate said with a frown. "Did I get the year wrong? Sorry. We had that McAleevy guy for Leaving Cert history. He was more interested in sneaking drinks from that hipflask he always carried than actually teaching us anything."

That sounded about right, Fiona thought—her sister, though smart, had managed to fail every subject in her Leaving Cert, including foundation maths which no one thought it was possible to fail. She was an even bigger waster than Ben, though she had taken to hair-dressing and now worked part-time at a salon in the town.

"It's not the year I'm bothered about," their mother said in that same ominous tone.

"Will I make tea?" Marty asked cheerfully, standing and bolting to the kitchen before anyone even had time to reply.

Fiona would have offered to help him, but she couldn't take her eyes off the confrontation. What was Kate doing? Surely she knew that referring to their mother's age never went well, let alone implying that she had come of age in the early nineteen twenties.

"Ah, I'm only messing, Mam," Kate said with a grin. "You're so easy to wind up. Now, Fiona, you were telling us how you met Robocop. Go on there. I want to do my eyebrows before I go to bed. Stop holding me up."

Fiona shot daggers at her across the table. So much for sisterly solidarity. Kate stuck her tongue out in response.

"Mam, are you going to let her away with that? She just insulted you for the craic. So cold-hearted! I worry she's a sociopath."

"Ye're all a bunch of sociopaths as far as I'm concerned," her mother shot back. "I'm used to it by now. Don't worry, she can cook her own dinners from now on and start paying me rent. Go on, Fiona. I've stuff to do as well but I'm dying to hear about your fling with Sergeant Brennan. All I can say is thank God he didn't want to make a go of things—imagine having him over here every night for his tea? We'd all go mad."

"Hey!" Fiona cried. "You assume nothing happened because *he* didn't want it to happen? After you spending hours of your life giving out about what an eejit he is? What must you think of me so?"

Her mother waved her hand. "I didn't mean it like that."

"What way did you mean it so?"

"Ah, don't be taking offence all the time."

"I'm not, I…" Fiona stopped. There was no point in even arguing, she knew. Only one person was allowed to take offence to everything that was said in the McCabe household, and Fiona supposed it was a fair trade—hearty meals in exchange for having to listen to her mother's frequent and very vocal outrage. "Fine. Okay."

"You'll tell us?"

Fiona took a deep breath. It was so long ago now that she wasn't sure where to start. It had been a regular night out with her friends from the office. They had gone to a few bars and then on to Coppers for a bit of a dance. Drinks had been had and the lighting in that place was low. And she'd met Sergeant Brennan. He had seemed nice at the time; polite even. He'd asked her to meet up again and she had agreed. Readily agreed. The memory filled her with horror—how had she not sensed his pure evil?

They had met for a drink the following week at a quiet little bar off Grafton Street. Sparks hadn't flown and Fiona had politely but firmly refused his request for a second date.

"And that's it," she concluded with a shrug.

"What do you mean, that's it?" her mother asked. "You two have been at each other's throats since he moved here."

"That's it. Think about it," Fiona sighed. "If there was a big drama then you'd have heard about it. As it was, I met him tipsy and very quickly decided I had no interest in another date."

"Why do ye hate each other so?"

That was an easy one to answer, Fiona thought. "I didn't hate him. I never gave him a second thought until he turned up here. It even took me a while to place him because it was years since our dull date. He recognised me immediately, though."

Her father had discarded his paper. Unusually for him, he had thrown it across the armchair behind him and seemed unconcerned by its messiness. "Please tell me this has nothing to do with the objection he put in to the council about the improvement at McCabe's."

"I wish I could," Fiona said with a sigh. "No, he's been after me since he arrived. All the speeding tickets and parking fines. All him."

"Why didn't you say?" Marty asked fiercely. "I could've gone and had a word with him; made sure he knew not to bother you again."

"He's a Garda," Fiona said quietly. "And not only that, but his father is high up. There was no point in worrying ye or making you all dislike him even more than you already did."

"But what did you even do to him? It doesn't sound like ye were attached to each other—it's not like you broke his stony little heart or anything," Mrs McCabe said, her hand resting on Fiona's shoulder. "Oh, love, you should have said. That's bullying, that is. I won't stand for it."

"Yes you will, Mam," Fiona said through gritted teeth. "Look, I have the dashcam now and he's eased off on the speeding tickets. I've contested them all anyway and never had to pay. He was just trying to get a rise out of me."

"Why bother, though?" Ben asked.

"Ego?" Fiona suggested, shrugging. "That's the only thing I can think of. I rejected him and he didn't like it. God, if I'd only known what I was getting into I would never have given him the time of day that night."

"You weren't to know," her mother said, patting her shoulder. "I'll make you another cup of tea, love."

"And I'll be sure to have the Land Rover handy the next time he's out for a walk and it's been raining," her father added ominously. "And I'll put my mind to thinking of other ways to get him. No one gets away with harassing a daughter of mine."

CHAPTER 13

Maybe it was the concern and sweetness her mother had shown her that evening that made Fiona relent, or it could have been a desire to form a new terrible date memory to replace her evening out with Sergeant Brennan. In any case, Fiona had found herself agreeing to meet up with her mother's friend Mrs Murray's son-who-was-back-from-Australia.

He'd gone to school in Newtownbeg and she couldn't remember ever meeting him. Her mother had worked with Mrs Murray in the bank after Fiona left secondary school, so there had been no playdates or other forced socialising. She wasn't able to track him down on Facebook either.

The absence of any memories or other pictures gave Fiona the freedom to imagine what he might look like. Naturally, the fact that he had lived in Australia for so long led her to assume that he looked like Chris Hemsworth.

She grew more and more excited as she waited for him at the bar in Treynor's in Newtownbeg. He had offered to come to Ballycashel but she had insisted. She had learned long ago that it was better not to go on dates within walking distance of her immediate family. There had been too many instances of them 'just happening to walk past' for it to be a coincidence.

"Can I get you another?" the barman asked her. She didn't recognise him.

"No, I'm fine for the moment, thanks."

"Waiting on someone?"

She nodded. "Yeah."

"I haven't seen you around here before. Have you just moved?"

"No, I'm from Ballycashel."

He sucked in a breath. "Terrible business over there. I heard ye had a murder!"

She nodded, not wanting to talk about it anymore but too polite not to answer his question. You couldn't do that in a place so close to home—they'd be calling her a snob before she even got home. "Yeah," she said noncommittally.

He didn't seem to notice her reticence—or if he did, he ignored it. "Terrible business. It was a local lad, yeah?"

She nodded. "It was."

"And a local fella who did it?"

Fiona was barely paying attention. "Nah, they reckon it was a fella from Dublin."

"A transplant, like?" He had abandoned the pretence of polishing glasses and was now leaning over the bar, seemingly intrigued by Ballycashel's crime.

She looked up at him, confused. "No, he didn't live there if that's what you mean. I'd never seen him before."

His eyes widened. "You were there? At the murder?"

"No," she said, shaking her head and beyond irritated now. "Of course not. I run a bar there. He was in that night."

"So you saw him."

"Didn't I just say that?"

"Okay, okay," he said, holding his hands up. "There's no need to bite my head off."

"Sorry." She shrugged. "I thought I was here for a drink, not an interrogation. I've never seen you in here before."

He reached for a cloth and began to haphazardly swipe at the bar. "This is only my second week. Do you come in here a lot?"

"Nah, not so much. Occasionally when I need a break from Newtownbeg."

"I know the feeling. This place gets claustrophobic too."

"You're from here?"

"Yeah," he said, nodding.

She frowned. "I've never seen you before."

He smiled apologetically. "Don't take this the wrong way, but we might have socialised in different circles. I just finished my Leaving last year. Jeff."

She laughed. "I'm Fiona. That explains it so. It's a damn sight more than a year since I finished mine. Are you going to college?"

"Hoping to," he said with a wistful smile. "I took a year out to save and do a bit of travel. I'm hoping to get into law. Missed it this year."

"Ah," she said, taking a sip of her drink. "That's why you're so interested in the Hanlon case."

He nodded enthusiastically. "I don't mean to be grim, like, but it's the first time anything like that has happened so close to home." He frowned. "Though, I'm surprised you say he's not local."

"Why do you say that?"

"Well the way it's laid out down there," he said carefully. "You'd never think it was the way down to the canal. I mean, I used to skateboard with my friends near there but we only knew about it because a lad from Ballycashel told us about it. It looks like the entrance to the carpark of the Garda Station. I don't know what it looked like before—maybe it's a recent thing… Anyway, there's no way a murderer is going to drag his victim down what looks like another entrance to a cop shop."

Fiona nodded. "That's true," she said, wondering why it hadn't struck her before. Maybe it would have if the identity of the perpetrator was still a mystery. "That Garda station has been there for as long as I can remember—you'd have to be local or someone who lived in town years ago to know about the layout. The lane doesn't show up as a road in maps. I'm sure that's one of the things they'll be asking him when they question him."

Jeff turned his head to one side. "What did he seem like?" he asked almost shyly. "Did he give you the heebie-jeebies when you saw him?"

She closed her eyes and thought back. Every part of her wanted to nod and say she had sensed something strange about him immediately, but the truth was he had just seemed like any other overly-impatient customer. "Not at all," she said at last. "He definitely didn't look like the picture I have in my head of a gangster. If anything, he…" she trailed off when she noticed his attention had been distracted. She looked behind her to see where he was focused.

And she couldn't help but smile. In fact, it was all she could do to stop her jaw from hitting the floor.

"How's it going, Jeff," the man said in a voice that was pure Newtownbeg with a distinctive Australian twang.

Fiona swallowed. Her mother had said David Murray was a good-looking fella, but then her mother tended to say that about every friend's son that she'd tried to set Fiona up with. Fiona had serious reservations about her mother's taste, but now she knew she'd judged too harshly.

He was built like a Greek god, tanned and strong-looking with mussed-up brown hair and thick black-rimmed glasses. And he was well dressed. Fiona prayed that this wasn't a cruel joke; that he wasn't some other guy from Newtownbeg who also happened to have returned recently from Australia.

"Can't complain, Dave," the barman said with a shrug. "We were just talking about that business over in Ballycashel."

"Fiona?" the Adonis said, tilting his head to one side as if trying to work out whether it was her. Fiona wouldn't put it past her mother to have provided an unflattering photo of her to Mrs Murray.

"Yeah," she smiled, holding out her hand. "David?"

"The very one."

By the time they had both ordered drinks and moved to the snug in the corner, Fiona was daydreaming about how she could ask Jeff to watch her pub while she and David Murray honeymooned in Australia and Fiji.

***

"Yeah, it's really cool," David said, taking a sip of his cocktail. "Getting to surf every morning before work is a dream for a lot of people, but my reality."

Fiona smiled despite the heartbreak she was feeling inside. How could someone so spectacularly good-looking be so... dull? "Lucky alright," she agreed, staring in dismay at her near-empty glass. There was no way she could have another drink and drive home, but this evening with David was making her want to march over to the bar and demand Jeff fill every available receptacle with something intoxicating.

"Well, you know," he said with a patient smile. "We talk about luck, but I feel like that diminishes my achievements somewhat."

"Is that so?" she asked, looking around for a distraction. Any distraction would do, she thought. Unfortunately, there were only a handful of other customers in the bar and they were all focused on the football match playing on the TV in the corner.

"I truly believe it is. I mean, I work hard and send so much good energy into the universe. Isn't it only right that I get positive things out of it?"

"Sure," Fiona said, enunciating exaggeratedly in order to mask a yawn. "Pity that doesn't work for people in Africa or the poor parts of Asia."

"Come again?"

He looked genuinely confused, she realised. Mrs Murray had always seemed like a nice lady whenever Fiona met her—how on earth had she raised a fella like this, with his head shoved so far up his you-know-what that he could no longer hear how ridiculous his own words sounded?

"Well, you say you got this great lifestyle and a high-paying job by sending out positive thoughts. It makes me wonder—all those people living below the poverty line must have sent out *bad* thoughts?"

He shrugged, still staring at her as if she was having some sort of meltdown. "I didn't say that, no."

"No," she said through gritted teeth as she wondered if she should just cut her losses and do a runner. "But... ah here, forget it," she said, waving her hand. "Here, do you think if I send positive thoughts into the universe I can have another glass of wine and miraculously not be over the alcohol limit?"

He puckered his lips in a way that brought to mind an unpleasant part of a cat's anatomy. "I feel like you're mocking me? I'd forgotten how negative Ireland is. People always trying to drag you down. All the naysayers—it's disheartening."

"I wasn't mocking you," Fiona sighed, pulling her phone from her bag and unlocking the screen under the table. "I was using your theory."

"All the same," he said. "It's alarming the dependence this country has on alcohol. Look here—we're meeting in a pub for God's sake." He waved his arms around as if to highlight the preposterousness of it.

Fiona paused. "It was your suggestion."

"Of course," he said, looking pained. "These terrible attitudes have been bred into me. Thankfully I've seen the light and cut out alcohol."

"What's that you're drinking then?" She nodded at his glass as she tapped a message to Marty. "It looks like a cocktail."

He smiled beatifically and shook his head. He reminded Fiona of one of those Head Boys from TV shows she used to watch as a child—infinitely superior in all possible ways, in his own mind at least. "It's pomegranate nectar and coconut water. About as far from a cocktail as you might get."

Fiona threw her phone back in her bag and nodded. "Sounds lovely."

"Do you want to try?" he asked, holding it out to her.

She stared at the bright pink mixture. "Are you sure? I might get my alcoholic aura and negative vibes all over it. I'd never forgive myself."

His face fell and she could tell he was searching for mockery. And then the uncomfortable silence was shattered by the non-descript musak of Fiona's ringtone. She pulled her phone from her bag and frowned at the screen.

"It's my business partner. I better get this."

David nodded.

"Hello? Martin? Is everything alright? I told you I was unreachable for the evening."

Marty cleared his throat. "Soz. We're in the middle of an emergency. Someone tried to force Mam to give up her soda bread recipe. Of course she refused as any good Irish mammy would but we have a bit of a standoff."

"Oh no, you're not serious?" Fiona said, forcing a pained expression and closing her eyes in a vain attempt to stop herself from laughing.

"I'm afraid so," Marty said. "And they've scheduled Dad in for surgical removal of his paper. So no doubt there'll be trouble in that quarter too."

"Ah," she said regretfully. "I'll be there as soon as I can."

"You're okay to drive?"

"Yes, yes, of course, more's the pity," she said, casting an apologetic look at David. "I'll see you soon."

"Everything okay?" he asked, after she'd ended the call.

She shook her head and pursed her lips as if she was filled with the deepest regret. "I'm afraid not. There's a burst pipe at the pub. I've got to get back there and start moving stock. Thanks a million for the drink."

She jumped to her feet and hurried out, relief swelling inside her.

CHAPTER 14

It was strange. Fiona got all the way back to Ballycashel and had parked in her usual spot. There was still no word from any of her family. Nor had any of them camped outside the door to her flat. She let herself in and hurried upstairs, expecting to find them all sprawled in her living room and ready to interrogate her about her date.

She had to admit, a small part of her was disappointed—for once, she had a good date story to tell. Well, a good *bad date* story at any rate. She had decided on the drive back that that was it—enough was enough. She wasn't going to allow her mother to set her up again.

Not that she ever planned it that way, of course. Mrs McCabe had a way of twisting her arm that meant she usually went from resistance to compliance over the course of a meal. And then all her mother needed to do was keep on hammering away.

"No more," Fiona muttered as she collapsed on the couch and flicked on the TV.

She considered calling her mother there and then and asking what on earth she'd been doing setting Fiona up with a narcissistic hippy, but she decided against it. She was exhausted. It was time for some guilty TV watching.

The first channel that came up was showing the nine o'clock news. Fiona reached for the remote. She was in the mood for bubble-gum TV—something vacuous like reality TV or a soap that didn't make her think too much. Before she could hit the button, though, she saw something that made her gasp in surprise.

It was Dec's killer, face plastered all over the screen.

Fiona lurched forward, staring at him. The picture looked like a still shot taken from high-quality video footage. He looked more aggressive and hostile than she remembered him. A shiver ran down her spine followed by a sense of immense relief that they'd caught him.

The murderer's picture disappeared and the shot returned to a TV presenter in the newsroom. Fiona had forgotten all about mindless reality TV now. She grabbed the remote and turned up the volume.

"Wanted in connection with a murder in the small town of Ballycashel. A witness provided Gardaí with a photofit image of the suspect, who was traced to an address in south county Dublin.

A Garda spokesperson confirmed that a man was arrested yesterday afternoon in relation to the offence."

"We've received reports just now that award-winning investigative journalist Simon Moriarty was the man arrested. He called our producers a short time ago after his release from Garda custody. Join us after the break, when we bring you an exclusive update on what seems to be a most unusual case of mistaken identity."

Fiona stared at the screen in horror as the reporter's words sank in. Mistaken identity? Her phone buzzed in her bag where she'd left it on the table. She didn't even have to see the screen to know who it was.

"You're watching the news, I take it," she said, after hitting the green dot onscreen.

"We are of course," her mother said. "We thought they were just announcing his arrest. What on earth is this about mistaken identity?"

"I have no idea. I just got home. I flipped on the telly and there was his face—the murderer's."

"What?" Mrs McCabe's voice grew muffled as she evidently turned away from the phone receiver to confer with her husband. "No, you must've seen something else. Your father heard the same thing as me—the murderer's at large."

"But I saw him," Fiona said, pointing futilely at the screen. "It showed a video still of him."

"Are you watching RTE1?"

Fiona had to check the little icon in the corner of the screen. She didn't often watch TV, preferring movie subscription services. "It is, yeah. I just switched it on before the ad break. It was him, Mam. A still from a video. He was in front of some big building or other."

"Fiona, love," her mother said, sounding concerned. "How many drinks did you have? That's no murderer. That's Simon Moriarty."

"But that's the guy who—"

"Shhhhh," Mrs McCabe hissed. "It's back on."

Fiona couldn't get a word out. She watched in confusion as the man from the bar walked out into the studio and took a seat at the table with the two presenters.

"That's him," she whispered faintly.

But her mother must have put down the phone because there was no answer.

"Good evening, Mr Moriarty."

"Alan," the murderer said. Fiona wondered why they'd brought him on the telly. Had they really believed him when he said he was a journalist? Had they not thought to check his credentials? It seemed extremely lax of them.

"Thanks for joining us tonight. I know you've just been through an awful debacle."

"That's right," Murder Man said grimly. "I wanted to share with your viewers so they know what the so-called peace officers in our country are capable of."

The presenter, Alan, nodded. "As many of you will know, Simon Moriarty is a reporter for the Sunday Saturn. He works undercover mainly, and has authored several books, mainly on the subject of crime. Can you tell us what happened to you a few days ago?"

The man nodded. Fiona found she was barely even breathing, she was so confused about the situation. She lifted the phone to her ear and listened—dialling tone. Her mother must have hung up.

"I heard a noise outside my home, and when I went out to investigate, I was met by armed Gardaí, who insisted on taking me with them. I have just spent the past several hours in an interview room, where I've had to justify my presence in a small village in Ireland on the night of a murder."

Alan, who had been nodding along with the story, grew serious. "That seems reasonable, I have to say. Don't they want to talk to everyone who was nearby and might have seen something?"

"Of course, Alan. That's exactly what they set out to do in cases like this. But this was no civil chat. They sent an armed unit to my house and the conversation flowed very much as if they believed I was the one behind the murder. So much for the presumption of innocence!"

Fiona's cheeks felt hot and fevered. She hit her mother's number and held her phone to her ear, cursing when she heard the engaged tone.

"And what *were* you doing in Ballycashel that night, Alan?"

The man smiled for the first time. "I was speaking to a source in relation to a story I'm working on."

"Is this of any relevance to the Garda investigation?"

"It might well be," Moriarty said, nodding sagely. "And I'll be happy to help them out when I receive an apology for their brutal, discriminatory treatment of me over the past twenty-four hours."

Fiona's phone rang as soon as the news segment ended and the sports presenter appeared on the screen.

"What's going on?" her mother wailed. "You never told me you have Simon Moriarty in the pub."

"I didn't know," Fiona sighed, head pounding with the beginning of a headache. What on earth was happening? "I'd never seen him before in my life. But that's the guy, Mam; that's the guy who was in the pub with Dec that night."

"What would Declan be doing talking to a journalist?"

Fiona shook her head and soon thought better of it. She massaged her temples. "I have no idea. None of this makes sense. It was him—the guards even said it."

"The guards," her mother snorted. "You know well how effective the guards are around here. I'm surprised they didn't blame it on El Niño or the Celtic Tiger."

"So what does that mean?" Fiona said looking around faintly. "If it's not him—and it certainly looks like it wasn't—then who was it?"

"Fiona." Her father's voice came on the line sounding even sterner than usual. "It's your father. I think in light of what's after happening you should stay here for the night. Let's see if we can figure out what's going on."

CHAPTER 15

Fiona only went home to humour them. That and the fact that she didn't really feel like being alone in the flat at that time.

"So if it's not him, it's got nothing to do with the pub then," she said, expecting to hear a chorus of agreement.

There wasn't a sound in the room.

"Unless the murder had something to do with the fact that he was talking to that journalist?" she suggested.

"Maybe," her father said. "Lookit, it's nothing to do with us. I know he was a friend of yours but your involvement ends now."

"I wasn't involved!" she protested.

"You were showing the guards the CCTV and you found that note from him."

"That's not being involved, Dad," she said, shaking her head. "He was last seen in the pub. Of course the guards had questions. Do you think I wanted to be stuck in close confines with Sergeant Brennan?"

"All he's saying, sweetheart," her mother said carefully. "Is don't be sticking your oar in now."

"I'm not."

"Yes you are. You're sitting there trying to solve the thing. Why don't you relax and have a cup of tea? I've the bed ready for you upstairs and you can borrow pyjamas off Kate. Lord knows she has enough of them to clothe an army."

"Fine," Fiona said weakly. "I was just curious, that's all. But you're right."

***

The decision to open the pub the next day was taken out of her hands, it turned out. Before anyone had risen in the McCabe household, there was a loud knock on the door. Fiona, asleep in the front box room, heard it first. She hurried out of bed and rushed down the stairs just as their early-morning caller began to knock again.

"I'm coming," she muttered, tying the waist of the fluorescent pink bathrobe that still hung on the back of her bedroom door.

She threw open the door, expecting to see the FedEx man who was a frequent visitor to the McCabe house thanks to Kate's obsession with buying makeup over the internet. Instead, she was met by the eager faces of the entire Ballycashel police force—all three of them.

"You're out early. Was there overtime going or something?" she asked, grinning as she anticipated the annoyed response from Sergeant Brennan.

"We tried the door of the flat. There was no answer. As a courtesy, we've come here."

"What's this about?" Fiona asked, stifling a yawn with the ragged flannel sleeve.

"We have a warrant to search the premises at 2 Mill Street, Ballycashel."

"That's my pub," she frowned.

"And the residential unit above it, yes," Sergeant Brennan said, clearly relishing the moment.

By now, her parents and two of her brothers had crowded behind her at the door and some of their early bird neighbours had stopped at the gate to rubber-neck.

"What's this about, Sergeant Brennan?"

"Here," he said, thrusting a sheet of paper at her. "You can read it for yourself. Now, I'll ask you to open the doors for us as a courtesy. Otherwise I'll be forced to break the door down."

Behind her, Marty snorted. "You? Break the door down? Are you going to do it with the force of your sense of entitlement or something?"

Sergeant Brennan ignored him. "You might want to get changed out of… that thing, whatever it is."

"It's a dressing gown," she smiled. "I suppose you haven't had much occasion to see women early in the morning so you wouldn't have known."

Garda Fitzpatrick snorted behind him, causing Sergeant Brennan to whip around and stare at him as if he was a naughty school child.

"I'll have you know that I have…" Sergeant Brennan stopped and flushed, realising that he'd let her wind him up and that everyone there knew it. "You have two minutes."

***

Fiona sat on the couch with her father and watched as the three Gardaí opened every drawer and cabinet in the place. They had already searched her bedroom and bathroom.

"Go easy with that cabinet, the drawers are delicate," her father growled.

She felt glad of the company. There was something extremely intimidating about having near-strangers poke around your home and having no way to stop them.

The search warrant was lawful—she had had no choice but to escort them back to the flat. By then, a large crowd of onlookers had assembled at the gate and some had even had the cheek to follow them to the pub. She glanced out the window. She had never seen Mill Street look so busy. She hoped it would provide a boost for some of her fellow business owners at least.

"Look, what's this about?" she asked for the fifth time. "I was nowhere near that murder scene. I showed you the CCTV footage. I was here long after he left the pub. This is a joke."

"We've had a tip-off that you—" Garda Fitzpatrick started.

"Shhhh," the sergeant cried. "You're not supposed to give that information to her."

"But sure it's probably nothing," Garda Fitzpatrick said, shaking his head. "I've known her since primary school and she's right—we saw that video."

"That means nothing," Sergeant Brennan snarled. "We haven't had our forensic people examine it."

"I see what this is," Fiona said slowly and deliberately. "You're embarrassed because you ordered the arrest of the journalist fella. Now you're taking it out on me. Is that lawful, Sergeant Brennan?"

"It seems it is if your father's a head honcho up in Garda headquarters," Francis McCabe said bitterly. "You'll be hearing from my solicitor, Brennan."

"No doubt I will if I end up arresting your daughter," Sergeant Brennan said snidely.

Fiona clasped her father's arm. He was used to his children messing and joking, but he wasn't used to this. Fiona feared that Sergeant Brennan's arrogant tone and insulting comments would cause her father to lose his temper and lash out at him. She wouldn't blame him, of course, but that was all they needed right now.

"Leave it, Dad," she murmured. "He's not worth it."

***

"I know my cooking's pretty poor," Fiona quipped as the Gardaí carefully bagged up the blender, mixer and slow cooker from the pub kitchen, as well as her oven trays and utensils. "But a murder weapon? That's a little far-fetched is it now?"

"This is appalling," her father added. "You've got a murderer out there and you three stooges want to play baker? Is this so you can make doughnuts down at the station, is it?"

"That's a very harmful stereotype, Mr McCann. Now, if you can't stay quiet, I'll have to ask you to wait outside."

"Why on earth are you searching my kitchen?" Fiona asked, shaking her head. They had done the same upstairs too. "I deserve an explanation at least. Declan didn't even eat here that night."

"We're just doing our jobs, Miss McCabe."

"Stop calling me Miss," she snapped, the tension getting the better of her. "It's Ms. I'm not eight and this isn't the eighteen hundreds."

"You'll have to keep your temper in check if you want to remain here for the duration of the search."

"How long more is it going to take?" she asked, glancing at the clock on her phone. "I need to get this place opened up for the morning."

"When you have the full power of the law behind you," Sergeant Brennan said, sounding sage. "Time is of no consequence."

Fiona rolled her eyes. "I assume there's an exception for those times when there's a crime in progress and time is of the essence?"

He shot her a look of utter disgust.

"Just tell me what you're looking for! What harm would it do?"

"Cyanide," Garda Fitzpatrick said, shooting her an apologetic look.

"Cyanide," Fiona repeated in disbelief, just as the sergeant yelled at Garda Fitzpatrick to shut up. "What on earth would I be doing with cyanide? You've been watching too much telly."

"My God, is there some sort of rule in this town where no one can keep a single fact to themselves? Garda Fitzpatrick, what did I tell you about keeping quiet?"

Fitzpatrick shook his head, looking defiant for the first time. "I didn't see the harm in telling her. We're searching her place after all. Sure it'll be public knowledge soon enough anyway."

"That's not the point. I'm your superior."

In name, anyway, Fiona thought. One glance at her father was enough for her to gather that he was thinking along the same lines.

"And you haven't even got the facts straight. It's not cyanide we're looking for, it's a substance that was administered to the victim which caused a reaction in his body that formed cyanide..."

"Wait a second," Fiona interrupted. "You're telling me now that you're not looking for cyanide. What is it you're looking for so? You think I baked it up?"

"Apple seeds," Sergeant Brennan said simply.

"Oh, fabulous. A wild goose chase," she said, rolling her eyes. "And you didn't think of having a look in the Prendergasts' fruit and veg shop first? Maybe you'll head there and look for beers and ciders, will you?"

Her father elbowed her. "Cool it, Fi," he whispered. "Though I agree with you completely."

She took a deep breath, closed her eyes and exhaled. Then she started to remember something. Her mother had always been fanatical about removing apple seeds when she made apple tarts. "They're poisonous, aren't they?" she muttered.

"That's right," Sergeant Brennan said as he got way too close to her beloved spice rack for her liking. She wished she was one of those paranoid people you see in the movies who go to great lengths to booby trap their own property. It might have at least given her some satisfaction from this farce.

"And you think I did it."

"As my staff member said against my orders, we received an anonymous tip-off from a concerned member of the public. That was enough to enable us to seek a warrant to search your premises."

"And you're looking for apple seeds," her father said, his voice dripping with sarcasm. "Should you not be investigating a murder?"

"Apple seeds in large quantities," Sergeant Brennan said silkily. "Can cause a reaction in the body that generates cyanide especially if they've been ground or smashed. Now judging from your menu, you have a lot of apple products. Plus—"

"Cider?" Fiona said incredulously. "I'm running a bar."

The sergeant cleared his throat. "Indeed. Well I also see that you offer apple Danishes some mornings."

"And that's a crime? So does every café the length of Ireland. Are you going to go harass them too?"

He ignored her. "You were known to the victim. It's feasible that you could have ground up enough seeds to poison him and put them in his drink undetected."

"You saw the video Sergeant Brennan!" she cried. "You saw me opening his bottles. There was no time for me to slip anything inside. You would have seen it."

"Of course," he said. "And you would have known that and tampered with the bottles earlier."

Fiona threw her hands up in despair. He had an answer to everything, it seemed, even if his answer made no sense. Though his words reminded her of something. She would have seen in the video if anyone had tampered with Dec's drink. No one had. That meant that whoever poisoned him had done it after he left the pub. Or before?

She pulled out her phone and tapped in *cyanide poisoning*. She expected her father to tell her to stop sticking her nose in, but when she looked up at him he simply nodded for her to continue. It was beyond nosiness at this stage, she realised. Her freedom might rely on them finding the real killer.

CHAPTER 16

There was a full complement around the McCabe's kitchen table, except for Mike who was in the States and Colm and Enda who were helping out with a pilgrimage to Lourdes (albeit reluctantly). They had decided not to bother telling the others—it was the middle of the night in Philadelphia and the other two were no doubt occupied with Granny Coyle and the rest of her friends on the trip.

"Right," Marty said, looking around. "Ye all know about the search at the pub."

There was a chorus of responses, varying from the enthusiastic/desperate (Fiona and her mother) to almost indifferent (Kate and Ben, who was forgoing a Playstation marathon with his friend Billy in order to attend).

"And ye also know that Sergeant Brennan has it in for me for reasons not so unknown," Fiona added. "So I thought we could sit down and look over everything we know. I've got my laptop hooked up to the telly, so if some of you could watch it at normal speed and really look out for anything strange that'd be brilliant. And that's basically it," she said, trying not to sound resigned. "Apart from the matchbook, there are no other clues. Not that we know of anyway. He was poisoned," she added in a quiet voice. "Apple seeds crushed up to form a powder that reacts in your body to form cyanide. Now, I don't know how accurate this is, but from looking on the internet it seems like the poison takes anywhere from two hours to six hours to work."

"Do we know his time of death?" Ben asked.

Fiona shook her head. "We don't. I asked the sergeant if I could see the files and he just laughed in my face."

"I'll go have a chat to Garda Conway," Marty announced.

"Nah," Fiona said. "Sergeant Brennan won't let you within ten feet of him. I've been trying to get information out of him since they started the search."

Marty's eyes twinkled. "Ah, but the sergeant won't be in Phelan's, will he?" he stood and pushed in his chair. "I'll be back as soon as I can, but I might be a while. I'll have to get old Garda Conway at least a few pints of the black stuff to loosen his tongue."

"Good man, Martin," their mother said, patting his arm as if he was off to pay tribute to the saints and not get a police officer drunk and shake him down for information.

"Yeah, that'll be a great help," Fiona agreed. "So yeah. That's it. All we know is it seems like he was poisoned after he left the bar; this useless message on the matchbook." She stopped and rubbed her eyes. The buzz of fear was beginning to wear off, leaving her more exhausted than she had ever felt. But something was niggling at her and refusing to be forgotten. "Ah, yeah. I was chatting to the barman in Treynor's in Newtownbeg. I didn't think much of it at the time because we thought it was the journalist fella, but now it makes sense. He said that he was surprised it wasn't a local because most outsiders wouldn't even know the lock existed. It's where it's located—you have to go round the back of the garda station to get down that lane and it's not marked on the map. No master criminal in his or her right mind would risk bringing their victim down there."

"What if it was Dec's idea to meet down there?" her mother asked.

Fiona leant back in her chair. "It's so complicated. We need that information from Garda Conway. Otherwise we have no idea of the time he died at and no hope of being able to work backwards. Right. Everyone have a look at this just in case and then we'll move on to watching the video. I've a pile of notebooks for us all and I want you to write down everything you see, no matter how trivial it might seem." She paused, expecting them all to give out to her for ruining their evening. No one did. Fiona found herself on the verge of tears. She fought with these people frequently, but they had her back and she had theirs. "Thanks, guys. I appreciate this. I owe ye one. I love you all, but don't tell anyone."

There was a chorus of groans, but they didn't descend into their usual chaotic messing and slagging. No, it was clear to everyone that there was a lot of work to be done and this wasn't a time for mucking around.

Fi passed the printed sheet to her mother, who was sitting next to her.

"Okay, now I was thinking. We still don't know why that journalist was here chatting to Dec. I'm kicking myself now for not trying to listen in on their conversation, but I didn't realise the importance of it. I'm guessing it was something to do with his time in jail, though. What else would it be? Now, it was either a coincidence that your man was here the same night as Dec was killed, or else he was killed because of it."

No one objected to her reasoning.

"Right," she said after pausing to see if anyone had anything to add. "So I'm thinking it might be an idea to give him a call and try to find out what he knows."

Mrs McCabe snorted. "What, you're just going to call up Simon Moriarty and say 'hi, how's it going. It's Fiona. Why were you in Ballycashel?'"

Fiona nodded. She'd been expecting a strange comment, but was surprised that her mother had simply summarised everything she wanted to say to the guy. "Yeah, that's exactly it. A longshot I know, but—"

"And you think he's going to talk to you?"

"I'm not sure, Mam, but I've got to try."

Her mother was shaking her head for some reason, not buying it at all.

"What is it?" Marty asked. "It might work."

"No," Mrs McCabe said. "No, it won't. He probably has women calling him up at all hours of the day and night. He'll have someone who answers his calls."

"Why would he have that, Mam? It's not like he's a big superstar or anything."

Her father spoke for the first time. "You'd be surprised. He's like the Daniel O'Donnell of the written word for some women of a certain age—I mean, some Irish women," he said hurriedly, looking hunted as his wife shot him a look of utter loathing.

"What?" Fiona howled. "I've never heard of him. Have any of ye?"

Her siblings all shook their heads.

"Ye wouldn't have, see," Francis McCabe continued. "Whereas this one." He pointed at their mother. "Her lot go wild for him. Ever since he did that expose about Fergus Conners and the banking scandal, he's been a hero for middle-class women over fifty."

"I am not over fifty," Mrs McCabe cried, folding her arms and looking utterly insulted.

Fiona glanced around the table. Her look said it all: *try not to laugh even though it's hysterical.* They couldn't afford to get distracted; not now.

It was too late, though. "Mam, Marty is thirty-six years old. You're telling me you were no older than thirteen when you had him?"

Fiona and her father sighed and threw their eye to the ceiling at the same time.

"*Now* you decide to learn maths?" Francis said, shaking his head. "I suppose I should be proud even if it did take you twice as long as the rest of them."

"Right, come on you lot," Mrs McCabe said, handing the printed sheet to Ben.

They all stood and moved towards the sitting room. Fiona had dragged the couch cushions onto the floor to make it comfortable for all of them to sit there. After all, it would take them several hours if they were going to watch the footage in detail at normal speed. She had stocked up the fridge with soft drinks and the presses with Tayto, and sneakily hidden all of the beer and whiskey in the shed. Now was definitely not the time to hit the booze—not if they wanted to stay sharp.

"It's the old Beetle," Ben said, showing no sign of moving from the table.

No one really paid attention.

"Come on, Ben," Fiona said, lingering at the door. "Let's get this over with. I'll make everyone a massive roast when this is all done."

For once the prospect of food didn't motivate him. He sat at the table, apparently rooted to the spot. He held up the sheet of paper. Fiona had never seen him look so concerned.

"Are you kidding me? You don't get what this means?"

Fiona sat down heavily on the nearest chair.

CHAPTER 17

"What are you talking about, Ben?" Fiona hissed, pulling the paper off him and staring at it expectantly as if its meaning was going to reveal itself to her now. She was disappointed to see the writing on the matchbook was as nonsensical as ever.

Ben smiled. "Don't you see?" he whispered, tapping at the sheet. "Remember the old car in Hanlon's field that ye used to use as a den?"

"What's that got to do with anything?" Fiona asked with a frown.

She remembered it well. A whole gang of children from the town had been drawn like magnets to the old car that was parked two fields back from Dec's parents' house. They had taken the back seats out and hung an old tarp they'd found from the trees, making a vast seating area. She couldn't imagine the pleasure in it now, but it had kept them occupied for days.

"The Beetle," he said, looking more animated than she'd ever seen him look.

"Yeah?"

"Don't you remember?" He stabbed the paper. "Danger. HQ. Dash. That's what you used to call it. Headquarters. HQ. Remember, I was really small and ye'd never let me come in until I went crying to Mam. What else do you think he's talking about? It has to be the car. We need to look in the dash; the glove box."

Fiona took the paper and stared at it again. Now that her brother had pointed it out, she wondered how they had all failed to miss it. "Brilliant, Ben. Thank God for your memory." Her eyes scanned over the message again. *Danger. HQ. Dash.* That had to be it. "I thought he meant dash as in hurry. But this… this makes way more sense."

He nodded. "It has to be the car."

"Come on," she said, hurrying to the door with the paper still in hand. "We've got to go check it out."

"But it's dark now," their mother said when they told her what they'd found. "You don't know who's out and about at this time. You don't even have a torch, do you?"

"I've a torch app on my phone," Ben said.

Fiona hesitated. "She's right," she admitted reluctantly. "We'll go have a look first thing in the morning. That way there's a better chance we won't miss anything." She heaved a huge sigh of frustration. "I suppose I better go call your man so."

"Let me do it," her mother offered, at which her father rolled his eyes dramatically.

"I'll have a daughter in jail for murder and a wife off gallivanting with some journalist fella who thinks he's a rock star."

"Dad!" Fiona hissed.

"Ah I'm only joking, honey. Well, about you anyway. Your mother'd be off with that fella given half the chance."

"I would not," Mrs McCabe said, shaking her head in disapproval. "No, it's better if I do it. I can butter him up; flatter the man. He'll think I'm one of his fans and then he'll feel bad if he hangs up without answering my questions."

"Mam, it's fine," Fiona said, scrolling through the Saturn website. There was no number listed for Simon Moriarty but there was a number for the newsroom. "They'll never put you through to him if they think you're one of his fans."

"And what, you're going to convince them you're ringing about something legitimate?"

Fiona nodded. "Exactly."

***

"Sunday Saturn," said a voice that was just warm enough not to sound disdainful.

"Yeah, hi," Fiona said, trying so hard to keep her voice low that it immediately hurt her throat and made her want to cough. "I'd like to talk to Simon Moriarty. I have some information he might be interested in."

"I see," said the woman.

Fiona waited, assuming she was going to be fobbed off and told to call back in the morning.

"Can I have your name?"

Fiona cleared her throat. "I'd rather not give it. I… uh… it could be dangerous if I share my identity."

"I see." There was a pause. "Hold the line."

Fiona looked around the empty room, fighting the desire to hurry back to the living room and tell them all 'I told you so'. There was no way she could do that and still maintain her composure.

"Simon Moriarty."

"Ah, hi, yes."

"Who is this?"

"I can't give you my name," she said, swallowing hard to stop herself from coughing. "It's in relation to one of your investigations."

"Oh?" he said. She caught the wariness in her voice.

"Yes," she wheezed. "Declan Hanlon. I have reason to believe that he was killed because of your visit to Ballycashel."

"Who is this?" he snapped. "I don't have time for this. Are you calling me with information or are you another rubbernecker looking to get off on this?"

"Neither," she admitted. "Look, I was hoping you could help. Dec was my friend. I want to know what happened."

"Well go to the Gardaí and ask them," he snapped, clearly wrong-footed. "I've told them everything I know." He hung up without waiting to hear her response.

Fiona opened the door and found her parents outside, heads suspiciously close to the door.

"You're up, Mam," she said, holding out the cordless phone. "He hung up on me."

"Okay."

"Do you want me to speak to the receptionist? She put me through last time."

Mrs McCabe shook her head and laughed. "No, love. I think I'll be just fine."

***

Fiona watched in amazement as her mother, who had always strongly disapproved of lying, grinned and told the receptionist that she had an awful tale of woe altogether and would she mind transferring her to Simon Moriarty so she could share it with him.

"She's transferring me," her mother hissed, holding her hand over the mouthpiece. "He probably thinks he's onto something that'll get him the Pulitzer."

Fiona shook her head in disbelief. "She always told me that lies are the devil's work."

"Course she did," her father said with a wry smile. "We have seven kids—how else do you think we might have maintained any semblance of control if ye were running around telling fibs? Ye were enough trouble as it was."

"I see," Fiona said, holding her breath as her mother nodded furiously.

"Oh, it's you, Mr Moriarty," she simpered. From the look on her face, she was enjoying this immensely. "Oh, what an honour. That report you did about those poor children." She sighed. "It was on my mind for weeks. You've a mastery with words."

She paused and listened. Fiona shot her a quizzical look which she completely ignored.

"Ah, would you go away out of that. Your mammy must be so proud of you. Is she still around?" Another pause. "Ah good. I bet she reads everything you put out and she couldn't be prouder."

Fiona gestured for her to get to the point. She was ignored again.

"Well, if you were *my* son, I tell you I'd have your picture up on the walls everywhere and no one would be able to walk into the house here without hearing all about your achievements. You're a credit to them."

Fiona gave up and just listened hard for any clue as to what he was saying.

Mrs McCabe laughed. "Well, I have seven and not one of them has given me cause to be, if you can believe it!"

Fiona was about to object but stopped herself in time. She looked around, wishing her siblings were there to share her outrage.

"I know, I know," she sighed with mirth. "Look, I'm calling you because—oh Lord, I don't even want to bring it up, it's such awful business. And the guards involving you." She closed her eyes and sighed. "A friend of mine, Mrs Hanlon; well her son was murdered here in Ballycashel. She's in a bad way. And sure the guards aren't interested—all they want to do is persecute good people like yourself."

By now, Fiona's hands were wet with perspiration and she had them clenched into fists to stop herself from shaking. This was it—if he didn't help them out now then there was no way they were going to get the information out of him, short of driving up to Dublin and bundling him into the boot of Marty's station wagon. And Fiona was pretty sure that might be considered kidnapping and slightly frowned upon.

"I know," her mother said softly. "A terrible carry on."

She was silent for several minutes and Fiona strained to hear. Was he telling her anything useful? Or berating her for wasting his time? She had wanted to listen in on the extension in the hall, but Mrs McCabe had forbidden her in case she made noise and alerted Simon Moriarty to the fact that there was more than one person on the line.

"I know she'd appreciate any information you could give us. A few of us have banded together—you know, from the ICA—and we're hoping to get to the bottom of it. Did he tell you of any trouble he was in? What about his time in jail—was there anyone after him? I don't know, maybe a drug lord he rubbed up the wrong way?"

Mrs McCabe listened and all the colour leeched out of her face quite suddenly. "What do you mean, you weren't talking to him about his time in jail? Wasn't that why you met him? For your story, like?"

Fiona inched closer. Mrs McCabe turned around so she was facing the other way.

"I see. Ah, I understand. Ah, I do. I wouldn't want to put you in an awkward position at all. Ah yeah, you've been very helpful. Give my regards to your mammy, won't you? Oh, bye. Bye, bye, bye."

Fiona grabbed her arm, but the line was dead by the time she got the phone.

"He didn't tell you anything? What did he say, Mam?"

"And what was that about the ICA?" Francis laughed. "You've never gone to that—you said it was for old biddies with too much time on their hands."

"Forget the ICA," Fiona hissed. "Mam, did he give you *anything*?"

Mrs McCabe pursed her lips and looked around at them severely. "Of course he did. He said he couldn't give away the reason for their meeting."

"Ah, not at all? Did you push him? If you'd have push—"

"Would you let me finish? He wouldn't tell me—he was adamant about that. But he did say it was nothing to do with Declan's time in jail."

"Oh," Fi said with a frown. "But what then…?"

"What indeed," her mother said, shaking her head. "He mentioned exposing something. Or someone. His articles are usually investigations into corruption; that sort of thing."

"You mean there's something going on in Ballycashel that was serious enough to call in a journalist? Why didn't Dec say anything?"

Her father cleared his throat and pulled off his glasses to clean on his shirt-tail. He didn't often get nervous and that was the only tell he displayed when he did. "The poor lad must have been in fear of his life. Whatever's going on had someone willing to kill him to keep a lid on it."

CHAPTER 18

Fiona glanced at the clock. It was almost nine and they were still watching the security footage from the evening of the murder. Their progress was slow—they had agreed it was best that they stop every half hour to discuss what they'd seen rather than go through a whole bunch of information and risk forgetting something.

So far they hadn't seen much.

Dec was in the bar. That was all. No one had approached him or even spoken to him except for Fi. She kept a close eye on Mrs Flannery, remembering the woman's scrutiny of Dec, though Fiona didn't really think the sweet old lady was capable of murder.

"Can't we fast forward?" Kate asked.

"No," Fiona and Ben said at the same time. Ben had become a lot more interested in their investigation since he'd solved the mystery of the matchbook.

"We've got to scrutinise it in case there's anything we missed," Fiona said. "I'll make you the best roast in the world, I promise. This is such a big help—no doubt they'll manage to fabricate something from my kitchen and make it look as if I did it."

"They won't get away with that," Francis said fiercely. "They'll have to put me in jail for what I'll do if they try and lock up one of my daughters."

Fiona smiled though her emotions were threatening to boil over. "Thanks, Dad. That means a lot."

"I mean it too," he said seriously. "I'd do anything for any of ye."

"Hopefully it won't come to that," his wife whispered, gripping his hand.

They were another half an hour through the video when Marty powered through the door. Everyone turned to look at him as if he had uncovered the secret of the Pharaohs.

"Don't get too excited," he said, holding up his hands. "I chatted to Steve Conway for hours. I don't think he knows much more than what we know."

Fiona felt like someone had stuck a pin in her and let all the air out of her body. "That was our only shot. He really knows nothing?"

Marty nodded. "Sorry, Fi. The only thing he could—or would—tell me was that the pathologist report estimated time of death at around two in the morning. We already knew the cause of death and where he was found."

"Ah," Fiona said, rubbing her tired eyes and trying to remember what she'd read online. "So that means he was probably poisoned between… em… eight pm and two in the morning?"

"That's what the guards think, but it's hard to be precise in these matters apparently," Marty said, throwing himself down beside her on the couch.

"So it's likely he was poisoned after he left the pub."

"Looks that way."

"So why the hell did they search the pub and my flat? It'd be different if they thought the poisoning had happened there."

Francis McCabe sighed. "I suppose they're grasping at straws what with having no suspects. They're probably under scrutiny for arresting your man Simon Moriarty too. Don't worry, Fiona. Nothing'll come of it, though it might make for an unpleasant few days. They have to try and pin it on someone after all."

Fiona shuddered at the thought. How far would they go? Would she see her face plastered all over the front pages of the papers like some actual murderer?

"But there *are* suspects. Everyone who was in the pub that night. Don't you see? It makes sense now. Only a local would have brought him to the lock.

"Come on, love," her mother urged. "I'll make another pot of tea and we'll keep watching the video. Something will come to us—you'll see."

***

Kate turned and grabbed at Fi so suddenly that she yelled out in fright.

"What on earth is going on?" Francis roared, grabbing the remote and pausing the TV.

"There! Look!" Kate pointed to the frozen image. "It's Will Connolly."

"So? He's nowhere near Hanlon."

"No," Kate said, hurrying over to the TV. "But look. Look at their hands and the way their heads are inclined. They're talking to each other. But it's obvious they're pretending not to."

They all leant closer and their father hit play again.

"Are they friends?" Fiona asked, remembering the strange look Will had given Dec in the bar that night. She couldn't remember seeing them talking. Sure enough, she appeared on the screen shortly afterwards to serve Will and both men noticeably turned their heads away from each other.

"I don't think so," Marty said. "I don't remember them ever hanging round together."

"Will is a quiet lad," Francis said. "Strong. I tried to get him into the hurling manys a time but he wasn't having a bar of it."

"Not playing hurling isn't a reflection on someone's character, Dad."

"Ah I know you say that, but it is a little bit. I don't trust people who won't play in a team. He was quite capable of doing it, you know."

"Maybe he didn't want to."

"Sure why wouldn't he want to? What else is there to do around here?"

They all looked at each other, stumped. "Hang around the corner?" one volunteered. "Play a musical instrument?" Fiona offered.

"I don't trust him. I think he did it," Francis said decisively.

And that was the end of that discussion.

Luckily, Gerry Reynolds chose that moment to appear on screen. "Now, here's someone who I actually think could have done it," Fiona said, chewing on the top of her pen.

Marty sat forward and watched. "He's a dodgy one alright. But it sounds like he has an alibi."

"Gerry? What was he doing?"

"Keeping tabs on him now, Fi? I don't know—Conway didn't say, just that they couldn't pin it on Gerry no matter how much they would have liked to."

"More Ballycashel justice," Mrs McCabe said bitterly. "You'd think they might have learned from what happened to poor Declan."

"Well if this journalist fella is to be believed," her husband said pensively. "It's possible that Declan's death had nothing to do with the time he spent in jail. I wonder what dodgy dealings he was into."

"Shhh," Kate hissed. "Look. Gerry's talking to Dec."

Fiona watched them closely. She had barely paid attention at the time nor when she had viewed the tape thinking Simon Moriarty was the killer, but now she found herself zeroing in on Gerry. It was strange. There was no hostility in his face; certainly not like there had been the day before the murder. Dec, too, looked relaxed. And from the way they were both gesturing, it looked like they were discussing something complicated.

"I wonder if Gerry knows what happened to him," Fiona said suddenly. "They seem to be on almost friendly terms."

"After the way Gerry was carrying on the day before?"

"I know," Fiona said, understanding the reason for her older brother's scepticism. "But look at them."

"I see what you mean," he said.

Shortly after, in a sequence Fiona could recite from memory now like the old boys on the radio talking about chess setups, Gerry left and Simon Moriarty took his place.

"No wonder you thought he was shifty Fiona," Mrs McCabe said. "It's remarkable how he kept his head down the whole time."

"I know, right? He made himself look suspicious even though he had a legitimate reason for being there. Well—so he says. I wonder if Dec knew he was coming."

"Rewind it there," Francis said. "Let's have a look."

"We'll never get through it at this rate," Kate grumbled. "I thought we were all supposed to be paying attention."

"It's important," Fiona said, trying to keep them all calm. "We'll all notice different things. Come on—we'll keep watching. Dad, I don't remember seeing Dec react weirdly to seeing your man so it seems like he knew he was coming."

"Why didn't he introduce you so?"

She shrugged, half paying attention. Her eyes were glued to the screen.

"There's Will Connolly again!" Mrs McCabe shrieked after they'd been watching in silence for a while.

"It is too."

"Ah, I remember that from the night. He really stared at Dec." She thought of something and it made her clap her hands together with excitement. "The orchard! Oh, I can't believe I didn't think of it. With all the apples he grows, he'd have access to hundreds of thousands of seeds if he wanted and no one would ever notice. Anyone else and it would have appeared strange, like why would they suddenly go and buy two hundred apples or however many you need to make a lethal dose?"

"Can't be," Marty said, deadpan. "Will played hurling."

Fiona was too distracted to laugh. She narrowed her eyes, willing herself to remember the exact details of Will's comments. The video was good, but it was grainy and in black and white. She shook her head. "All I remember is him staring. He was asking who the guy with Dec was."

"It must be him!"

They lapsed into a frenzied sort of silence: every one of them was fidgeting with a pen or messing with something or other.

"Did ye see that?" Francis bellowed, causing Fiona to almost jump out of her skin.

"See what?"

"There! That!" He was off his feet and jabbing at the screen. "Rewind it!"

"We're watching it through," his wife muttered. "There's nobody there."

"But there is! Go back! The door opened."

Fiona rewound back a minute or so and they waited. She slowed it down to half speed and sure enough, you could just about make out the door opening to the extreme right of the frame.

"No one left, though," she said. "We'd have seen them. And no one new comes in until the hen party arrives. I remember that."

"What was it so?"

No one had an answer.

CHAPTER 19

It tasted like something had rotted in her mouth. Fiona sat up, blinking around the room. From the looks of it, she wasn't the only one who had simply fallen asleep where she'd been sitting. Marty was sprawled out on the ground and Ben was stretched across the other couch. Neither was stirring. She stood and shuffled to the kitchen to get a drink.

She was surprised to find her mother already up. Mrs McCabe rarely rose before eight and it was just gone six at that point.

"What are you doing up?" Fiona asked, coming up behind where she stood at the cooker and leaning over her shoulder. "Pancakes! What's the occasion?"

"I thought you could use every bit of strength you could muster. It's been a stressful few days." Mrs McCabe turned and smiled with a tenderness Fiona wasn't used to seeing.

"Thanks, Mam. I appreciate all the help."

"Of course, love," she said, rubbing Fiona's arms with her warm callused hands. "Anything we can do to support you, you just name it. It's terrible them searching you like that. Psychological games, they call it. And you doing nothing wrong."

"Ah, I know." She paused. "Is breakfast far off?"

Mrs McCabe looked at her like she was mad. "It's not even seven in the morning. Where are you thinking of going at this hour?"

"The old Beetle. Remember, we were talking about it last night. Dec left a note about it—we should check it out."

Her mother looked sceptical. "Are you sure it's not one of Ben's funny notions?"

"I think so," Fiona said, biting her lip. "I mean, it's not beyond the realm of possibility, but it makes sense. If Dec didn't feel comfortable just talking to me, then maybe he didn't feel right handing a bunch of documents to one of us. He had to do it secretively."

"Documents?" Mrs McCabe didn't look up from flipping pancakes.

"Well, yeah. I assume so. What else could it be?" Fiona sighed. She was just after realising she had no idea what they were dealing with. "I don't know. It feels like the only thing we can do. We owe it to him to at least look."

"And if you don't find anything?"

"Well then it's back to the drawing board."

"Do me one favour, pet," Mrs McCabe said, expertly flipping one pancake onto a plate and grabbing the jug of batter. "Wait until it's bright and don't go out there alone. Make sure you take the lads with you. And your sister, though God knows she's not much use to you."

Fiona leant against the counter and stared at her. "You think we're onto something, don't you? Something serious?"

Her mother wouldn't meet her eyes.

***

Finally, after what felt like hours, Fiona, Marty and Ben left the house. The sun had come up— not that you could really tell. The light was dark blue and faint, but at least it wasn't raining. They had decided to walk instead of driving, just in case there was anyone around who might take exception to them going onto the Hanlons' property.

For all their mother had talked on the phone about her friendship with Mrs Hanlon, the truth was there was no one in that family to worry about tracking down Dec's killer. Mrs Hanlon had been sent to live in a home the previous year and her husband had already been in there for several years. Both were frail and unable to take care of themselves anymore. A group from the village had decided against even telling them about their son—as far as they were concerned, he was still a mischievous eight-year-old boy.

They had thought about contacting a cousin or aunt about going onto the land, but decided against it for fear of causing a fuss. Fiona was beginning to doubt that they'd find anything in the car—she suspected they'd all been carried away by hysteria and lack of sleep.

The Hanlon house was a twenty minute walk out of town and it took them another few minutes to get onto the land and make their way through the fields to the car. Back when they were kids, there had been an old house not far from the car. It had belonged to Dec's granny, as had the Beetle. The house was long gone now: even back then it had been overgrown and stuffed to bursting point with creeping plants. Now it was little more than a patch of disturbed grass.

The car—much to their surprise—looked much as they remembered it. At least, it did from two hundred yards away at the gate.

"Right," Fi said, climbing over the gate and marching ahead. "Let's check this out and get out of here as fast as possible."

Being there was giving her the creeps. She didn't know why and she didn't want to think about it for longer than she needed to.

"Oi!"

All three of them spun around. It wasn't clear where the voice had come from.

"What are you doing here?"

Fiona turned. She had spun in the direction of the gate they had climbed over and now she realised that the person was standing at the gate opposite it on the other side of the field. The car lay roughly in the middle.

"Who's that?" she muttered.

Marty stalked forward. "I don't know. I can't see his face but it looks like a shotgun he's carrying."

"Oh my God," Fiona hissed, startled. "What the hell is going on?"

"Yeah, what is this? A horror movie?"

"Calm down, Ben," Marty whispered. "Stop imagining things. He could just be out hunting." He cleared his throat and walked towards the man. "Hi, how's it going? We're just out for a walk."

The man was getting closer and closer. Fiona was relieved when she saw the gun was slung over his right arm and pointing towards the ground.

"What are you doing here?" he called.

She recognised him now—Marty obviously did too. "Pete! What are you doing here? You scared the bejesus out of us. Thought you were some mad old uncle of Dec's."

Normally, they might have expected a fellow Ballycashel resident to stop and have a chat; to at least crack a smile. But Pete Prendergast didn't slow his pace one bit.

Fiona didn't like this at all. "Come on," she muttered out of the side of her mouth. "Let's go."

They were still a bit away from the car, but something made her not want to draw his attention to it. Her brothers understood.

"What are ye doing here?" he asked, when he was within twenty yards of them.

"Just out for a walk, Pete," Fiona said, smiling widely. "How about yourself? Mary not with you?"

"What are you doing here; I asked you before?" he snapped. Up close his face was strained and lined. "This is private property."

Fiona frowned. "We're just walking through to the stream. It's never been a problem before."

"And what the hell are you lot planning on doing down there?"

Ben stepped forward and Fiona prayed he wasn't going to give the game away. "We're going to have a little memorial service for Dec. He was a friend of ours."

Fiona could have hugged him: it was perfect. But Pete didn't seem swayed by their sweet little cover story.

"He's gone," he said nastily. "He won't appreciate it. Go on—get off my land."

Marty moved as if he was going to go for him. Fiona hurried forward and grabbed his elbow. "Come on," she whispered. "We'll just go."

Marty ignored her. "Since when is this your land? This is Hanlon's field."

"It's mine," Pete said, glowering. "I bought it."

Fiona's eyes were glued to the shotgun. "Come on, Marty. We'll head away. We can have our little farewell thing further along the stream."

"Aye, right," Pete said, eying them all. "'Tis better you do that alright."

Marty continued to square off to him for another couple of seconds before backing down. "Ah, alright. Come on. We'll go." He turned towards the gate in the far corner and stopped as abruptly as he'd started. "Are you out shooting pheasants, Pete? I might have to join you someday."

"Aye. Not many about though. I'll have to look elsewhere."

They all muttered goodbyes—more because of the gun than because of any sense of affection—and headed across the field.

***

"Well, what now?" Ben muttered as they marched down the road. "We can't get to the car if he's wandering around shooting birds all day."

"Garda station," Marty said.

"We can't very well go and ask them to escort us to the car, can we?" Fiona said, hurrying to keep up. "And if we tell them about the car then we won't get to see what's inside. Marty, if Dec wanted the guards to see it he would have told them."

"I know all that."

"Well then why go to the guards? Look, we can wait until later when he's done shooting. What time do they stop at? Dusk?"

Marty stopped walking and turned to them both. "I'm not going to the guards so we can give them whatever's in the Beetle," he said with a strange smile. "I'm going to them because there's an armed maniac keeping guard over that field for some strange reason."

"You said he was probably hunting."

"That's what I thought."

Fiona sighed. "He said that's what he was doing. He's looking for pheasants—not finding them either, it sounds like."

Marty shook his head. Fiona was not comforted by the look in his eyes—he seemed haunted. She was used to her big brother being the most chilled out, reasonable one in the whole family.

"What's going on, Marty? Something's bothering you big time."

He wiped his face. "I don't know why I even said it; I guess I had it in mind to try and catch him out. I never expected…"

"What?!" Fiona cried. "What's going on?"

"No one goes hunting pheasants at this time of year," he said quietly, looking all around him as if he feared being overheard. "And if you were going hunting, you damn well wouldn't tell anyone. It's out of season. Big fines for anyone caught."

"What are you saying?"

"He's lying, Fi. There's no way he'd admit to shooting pheasants out of season. For all he knows, I could be straight on to the guards. I don't know him well, but I know he's not stupid."

"So what was he doing out there with a gun?" Ben gasped.

"I don't know, but I have a feeling it's got something to do with Dec and that note."

CHAPTER 20

The walk into town had never felt so long. They were all jumpy, expecting someone to leap out at them from behind one of the overgrown hedges that lined the narrow road. No one did, though, and soon they emerged onto the wider road that led into the town.

A car whizzed past them going way over the speed limit. Luckily there was a proper footpath now, otherwise Fiona feared they would have been hit. When she saw the familiar orange Prendergast's Greengrocers sticker on the rapidly shrinking vehicle, she let out a squeal.

"I think that's Pete's car! I recognise the sticker on the back."

Marty looked at her and then at Ben.

"No," she said. "It's too dangerous."

"He's just driven past us," Marty said. "We're not far from home. I can be at the house and in the car before he even knows."

"He'll shoot you," Fi cried.

"He won't get near me." Marty turned to Ben. "Have you got your phone on you?"

Ben nodded.

"Great. Fi, you go talk to the guards. Try and get Fitzpatrick and not that Robocop eejit. Tell him. Ben, you stay right here. I'm going to run home and get the car. If you see him drive past— it's a navy Corolla, right Fi?"

She nodded.

"If you see a navy Corolla go past you ring me straight away. Okay? Just hang around at the bus stop up there; pretend you're waiting for the bus to Dublin."

"It doesn't come until the evening," Ben said sceptically.

"Well *pretend*. You don't need to actually get on the bus. Just keep watch. Can you do that?"

Ben nodded.

"Right." Marty looked at Fi. "We've got to have a look inside that car. It'll be grand. Pete just drove past us and probably saw us walking back towards town. He's not going to expect us to go back there."

"Okay," she said with a sigh. "Are you sure we should tell the guards?"

"No," he said. "How about you hang back until you hear from me?"

"But what if he shoots you in the meantime? Maybe I should get them to go out to the car?"

Marty clicked his fingers. "I have it. I'll stick in my headphones and I'll keep talking to you as soon as I get out of the car to go look at the Beetle. You stick close to the Garda station and if I give you the signal or if I stop talking to you, get in there as fast as your legs can carry you."

She nodded. "This actually sounds like it might work."

Marty had already taken off across the road and down a narrow street that led—via a series of other streets—to their house.

***

Fiona felt very conspicuous sitting outside the deserted ice-cream shop across the street from the Garda station. It was April in Ireland—nobody in their right mind would venture out for ice-cream. In fact, the only reason the little shop stayed open was because its owners had set it up as part of some complicated tax dodge. Still, the ice-cream was nice and more importantly, it was the only place with outdoor seating where she could sit and watch the station. After all, she was apparently a suspect in the case, so she didn't want the gossip mill of Ballycashel doing any more speculating about her.

She carved off a small spoonful of orange sorbet and tried to stop herself from shivering as it melted in her mouth. She stared at her phone. Marty hadn't called her yet and she was starting to get worried. She unlocked the screen and stared at the bars. She had full reception and it was likely that Marty had too—there were enough cell towers in the vicinity to make sure of it.

"Is anyone sitting here?" a voice growled.

Fiona looked up and found herself face-to-face with Gerry Reynolds. "No," she said, willing him to leave her alone. She usually had no trouble speaking her mind but that didn't extend to thugs like Gerry Reynolds.

"Lovely morning," he said, hands in pockets. At least the small cup of chocolate chip ice-cream he was ignoring was in no danger of melting in the arctic wind. It sat there abandoned, spoon still shoved in the top.

"Just gorgeous," Fi said, telling herself not to be so sarcastic to a fella who was probably a murderer. She froze. What if this was his way of intimidating her into silence?

He laughed. "Terrible business with Dec Hanlon."

The blood ran cold in Fiona's veins. "Awful," she said quietly.

"I was there that night."

"You were what?" she hissed, before getting a grip on herself. "Oh, yes. In the pub." Her voice sounded like a robot's: unnatural and stilted.

"Yeah, of course in the pub. What, do you think it was me who murdered him?" He gave her a big leery grin.

Fiona squeezed her lips between her teeth and shook her head. As she did so, she took stock of her surroundings. Martha, the student who worked in the ice-cream shop, was all of five foot nothing. She'd be no help. The shops on either side were run by older women, who she couldn't imagine being much use against Gerry Reynolds. No, her only option was the Garda station across the road if Gerry decided to attack. She stared at her phone, willing Marty to call. What if he tried to reach her when she was in the station?

I could tell them it's an emergency, she thought.

"You're very quiet. You're normally the life and soul of the party," Gerry said, squinting at her.

Fiona's stomach lurched. Had he been watching her? Was he going to try and kill her? "My brother's coming to meet me here," she said quickly.

"Ah lovely," he said, his smile not meeting his eyes. "Bit of quality time with the family."

"Are you not eating your ice-cream?" she asked, mainly to fill the silence.

He glanced at it as if he'd never seen it before. "Nah. I'm not a big fan of sweet things."

Fiona's stomach lurched. "I have to go. Do. My. Passport photos," she yelled, getting up in such a hurry that she almost knocked orange sorbet all over the table.

Clutching her phone, she raced across the road, barely stopping to check if there were cars coming. She hurried up the steps to the Garda station, afraid to look back to see where he was in case she slowed down and it allowed him to catch up with her.

"Watch where you're going!" someone snapped.

"Sorry," she said absently, hurrying past. She looked up and baulked. It was Pete Prendergast.

"You ought to be."

She forced her legs to move; to get inside the doors of the station. Thankfully they cooperated. She rushed inside, lungs screaming for air. She needed to do more cardio, she knew—that's if she survived all this.

CHAPTER 21

Garda Fitzpatrick was behind the desk. She could see Sergeant Brennan in his office. The door was open.

"Can I...?" she asked the guard without stopping to hear his reply. She'd have much rather dealt with Fitzpatrick, but he wasn't the most pro-active. She'd rather talk to Sergeant Brennan than wind up dead. She glanced at her phone—Marty still hadn't called.

She stopped in her tracks and dialled his number. To her relief, he answered on the first ring.

"Fi," he whispered.

"Are you alright? What's going on?"

"I'm grand. I'm on the way home. I found an envelope. We can look at it at the house."

"Are you mad?" she hissed. "I told you to call me. That was our plan."

"Ah, Fi," he said. She could hear the smile in his voice. "I got there and realised how silly that was. There was no one around. And sure, I'd take

180

on anyone that came at me. Ben never called. Everything is fine."

"This isn't a phone box, Miss McCabe," a cold voice said.

"Gotta go," she muttered. "See you back at the house."

She hung up and spun around. "Sorry," she said, not meaning it. "Urgent business."

"I'm sure it was," he said with a smirk. "Now, what can we do for you?"

She stared at him, suddenly getting the feeling that she was being shoved backwards down a tunnel at high speed. "We weren't trespassing," she said hurriedly, not meeting his eyes. She didn't want to grovel, but she knew he'd throw the book at her if she was found in the wrong. "We were just going for a walk."

Sergeant Brennan snorted. "And I'm supposed to be interested in your leisure activities?"

She froze. This wasn't what she'd expected. But if Pete hadn't gone to report them, what had he been doing at the Garda station? She glanced at Garda Fitzpatrick through the open door. Maybe he'd been renewing his gun licence, she thought. Still, something about the situation filled her with unease.

"Well?" Sergeant Brennan said.

"It's Gerry Reynolds," she said hurriedly. "He just tried to intimidate me in the ice-cream shop. I think he might be involved in Dec's murder."

"That's quite a leap."

She shrugged. "Not really."

"Perhaps you're just trying to take the heat off yourself?"

She shook her head. "I had nothing to do with it—you should know that by now. Have you not got the lab tests back?"

He pursed his lips and watched her coldly. "They came back clean."

"Why didn't you tell me?"

"Because," he said slowly. "You had ample time to wash away the evidence. Don't think you can pull the wool over my eyes."

"I'm not! I wasn't involved. You've got no evidence against me."

He sighed. "If it's out there, I'll find it. Now. Tell me more about Gerry Reynolds."

She moved to take a seat in front of his desk and then thought better of it. She stood in front of him. "He was in the pub the night Dec was killed. And he just followed me to the ice-cream place and made it very clear that he was only there to intimidate me. He was asking me about the case. I think he thinks I know something."

"And do you?"

Fiona remembered Pete's hasty departure from the Garda station and hesitated. "No," she said. After all, she had no idea what Marty had found in the Beetle.

"Well then you should be fine."

"Oh, that's great. Thanks. I'll let my family know to sue you if he murders me too."

She turned and marched out of the office, resisting the urge to slam the door.

"How're you, Fiona?" Garda Fitzpatrick said from behind the desk.

She smiled and nodded. "Can't complain. And yourself?" She thought of something and walked over to the desk.

"Ah, grand now. It's cold all the same."

"It is," she said, mind working furiously. "Here, Garda Fitzpatrick. Did I just see Pete Prendergast come out of here?"

He nodded.

Her heart raced. "And did he say where he was going? It's just I wanted to talk to him about his bar tab. Would you know where I can find him?"

"Ah sorry, Fiona. I have no idea. He came marching in here and went straight to the sergeant's office. They were in there for over half an hour. Blinds down and everything." Noel Fitzpatrick tutted like it was outrageous carryon.

"You'd swear they were being filmed for the telly or something."

It took all the effort Fiona possessed to get her legs to work and carry her out of the station.

***

"Where did you get to?"

Fiona had hurried back to the end of the street and turned left onto Church Street. She spun around even though she recognised the voice. Why wouldn't she? She'd been talking to him not fifteen minutes before.

"Gerry," she said, trying to smile. "Fancy meeting you again."

He glowered back at her.

She looked around. It was typical—the town was usually busy on weekday mornings, but now it was empty. Worse still, most of the shops on that stretch of the street were closed or unoccupied. She'd never make it back to the pub. No, she was done for.

Desperation did away with the last bit of self-control she had left. "Were you following me, Gerry? What do you want? I don't know anything about the murders; I swear!"

"I was," he said simply, eyes everywhere except on hers.

Does that mean he's going to kill me and he feels guilty? Hardly—he's a hardened criminal. Unless… he feels guilty and does it anyway.

"Get away from me!" she cried, wishing there was someone in their vicinity who might hear them. "If you hurt me I'll come back and haunt you."

"I'm not going to hurt you," he growled reaching for her arm. "I just want to talk to you."

She pulled away just in time and managed to stay out of his grasp. She stared at him. He was tall with a lean frame, but years of drinking had given him a pot belly. She didn't usually give him much thought, but now she tried to assess what that meant for his fitness. She'd seen him out the front of Phelan's smoking, but what did that mean? Mike had smoked for years and he'd always been one of the fastest players on the pitch.

She looked around. The street was still deserted. She made a decision then. She'd try to talk him down and if there was the slightest hint that he'd try to attack her, she'd run for her life and go to the guards.

"Jaysus, what's gotten into you?"

"I dunno," she said, fighting the urge to roll her eyes. "Might be something to do with the fact that someone's after me."

"That's what I wanted to talk to you about."

"It is?" she asked warily. "So we're just being open about this, are we? You're hunting me down and you're all chilled out about it?"

He grimaced. "I'd hardly say I was chilled."

Oh my God, Fiona thought. *I'm dealing with a psychopath here.* Out loud, she said: "I don't mean to be condescending, but have you ever thought about getting help? You know, if you didn't feel like admitting anything to the guards you could always talk to Father Jimmy or Doctor Grimes, you know?"

He reddened. "You really think it's a problem? Jeez, Fiona, I wasn't expecting that reaction." He stepped forward.

At that moment, a car rounded the corner. Fiona waited until the last possible moment before dashing in front of it. She heard the sound of squealing tyres and frantic beeping, but she didn't look around or slow down until she'd run all the way back to her parents' house.

CHAPTER 22

"There you are," Marty said, looking impatient. "I've been waiting for you."

"Waiting?" she gasped, her breath jagged. "Waiting?" Gasp. "I've just." Gasp. "Had Ger—" Gasp. "Threat—" Gasp. "Kill me."

You could have heard a pin drop in the McCabe's front room. They all stopped what they were doing for a moment before a cacophony of voices started screaming at her.

"One at a time," Fiona sighed, picking up Kate's water bottle and gulping down the pint or so that was left in it.

"Gerry Reynolds just threatened to kill me," she said, looking around at them all.

"What? Where is he now?" her father paced the room, muttering to himself. "Is he out there? Have you called the guards?"

"No. It was on Church Street. A car came and I legged it. I don't know where he went—I didn't look back to check."

"Good girl," her mother said. "I'm ringing the guards. I know Brennan is an awful eejit but that Gerry fella needs to be locked up. What did he do?"

Fiona shook her head. "Nothing. He tried to grab me, but I got out of his way. He admitted to following me and said he was out to get me. I wasn't sure I'd get away so I thought it was best to try and calm him down. When I suggested he talk to someone he got even madder. Then I ran for it."

"Jesus, Mary and Joseph," Francis McCabe muttered. "I'll kill him so I will. My only daughter."

"Here," Kate bellowed. "What about me?"

"It was a figure of speech," their father said. "Right. Marty? Are you right?"

Mrs McCabe rushed to her husband's side and Fiona shot a warning look at her brother. "You'll do no such thing."

"See? I'll call the guards."

"No," Fiona said, shaking her head. "You won't do that either."

"What, so we're just supposed to let Gerry kill you?"

Fiona shuddered. "No, that's not ideal either. But we can't go to the guards. I just saw Pete Prendergast there. He was in with the sergeant for half an hour. I think Sergeant Brennan might be involved in this somehow."

"He's not," Marty said, more decisive than she'd ever heard him.

"But I just saw Pete in there. Remember Pete? Who tried to get us with his shotgun?"

"Not him," Marty said.

"But the pheasants and the gun and him running to the sergeant. Oh yeah, and the sergeant knew nothing about us being on Pete's land. So what were they talking about? And Gerry's involved too apparently. Why else who he want to kill me?"

She shivered as she remembered Gerry's questions about Dec and the journalist. He must have remembered that conversation. What if she was the only loose end that could tie him to the crime? She groaned in terror.

"Would you both shut up about Pete and Sergeant Brennan?" Francis hissed. "Who cares? There's a madman after Fiona. Now, if you won't go to the guards, you're leaving me with no choice but to get my gun from the room and go out there and find him myself."

"Oh God," Fiona groaned. Talk about being between a rock and a hard place: neither choice seemed particularly appealing to her at that moment.

"I'm not joking with you. Nobody messes with my family. Who does he think he is anyway, with that stupid moustache and that ridiculous haircut?"

***

"Do you realise you look like a crowd of hooligans off to a football match? Ah Francis, for the love of God will you let it go?"

"No, love," Francis McCabe said in a calm clipped voice that seemed utterly at odds with the hurley he brandished as a weapon.

Fiona rolled her eyes. "At least we convinced him to leave the shotgun."

"Don't laugh: this isn't funny."

"Sure there's nothing I can do about it. I tried to make him see sense."

"Come on lads. Are ye ready?"

The McCabe lads nodded their agreement. Both of them stood in the hallway. Marty held his hurley and Ben held the cricket bat that was bought at the height of Colm's brief foray onto the cricket bandwagon after Ireland beat England in the cricket world cup.

Ben opened the front door.

"Ah stop it, would ye? I'll never be able to show my face in town again after this. We'll have to move to a caravan by the side of the road."

"I've never been so mortified in all my life," Kate said, bolting up the stairs and slamming the door of her bedroom.

"Please, Dad," Fiona begged. "Just leave it."

"And what then? What if he tries to come after you again?"

She shrugged helplessly. "I'll carry a knife in my handbag. I don't know. Maybe we won't have to worry about it when he gets arrested—he's obviously involved in this whole Dec business."

"About that," Marty said. "You need to see what I found—"

"Come on," Francis McCabe bellowed. "No child of mine is going to be left too afraid to walk the streets in her own town."

"I told you—I'll get a knife."

"Oh, don't be silly, Fiona. You have the coordination of a baby deer. Remember when I took you to the Irish dancing in the hall? You're more likely to injure yourself than anyone else."

"Oh for God's sake!" Fiona cried, barrelling forward and slamming herself against the door. "Now! You'll have to go through me if you want to get out there and I'm not budging."

Her father looked nonplussed for a moment before he simply turned and walked through the house.

"Back door," he barked. The others hurried after him.

***

"I thought you were dead against going after Gerry," Ben said as they marched through the town. Net curtains fluttered in every window they passed.

"I am," Fiona said, trying to pretend that no one was watching and judging them.

"That's a pretty handy weapon for a pacifist."

She clenched the hurley handle tighter. "I'm not a pacifist. I'm just opposed to my entire family acting like some kind of vigilante militia. I'm only here so I can talk some reason into Dad before something awful happens."

"Well, you said yourself that we can't trust the guards. What else are we supposed to do? We can't have Gerry Reynolds threatening to hurt you. You're a pain in the ass but you're *our* pain in the ass."

Fiona pulled her younger brother into a bear hug, being careful to avoid hitting him with her stick. "Thanks. I don't want to even think about what the neighbours will say, but thanks for having my back."

"Always," he said, before breaking out into a huge grin. "Now, enough of this sappy stuff. Let's find Gerry and make sure he knows there'll be hell to pay if he so much as looks crooked at you again."

***

It didn't take long to find him. Gerry Reynolds kept an office of sorts in the back booth in Phelan's. Luckily the pub was half-empty when they walked in.

"Francis," Jimmy the owner said with a nod. He was used to seeing the lads come in after hurling training on Tuesday evenings, so he passed no remarks on the hurleys. His eyes lingered on the cricket bat, though.

"Jimmy," Francis muttered, scanning the bar and zeroing in on Gerry in his usual spot.

Gerry looked up before anyone spoke—he must have sensed the tension in the air and known it was directed at him. Fiona lingered behind them wishing she'd said nothing at all.

"Mr McCabe," Gerry said, dropping his newspaper.

"Gerry."

Fiona cringed as her father lifted his hurley and smack it into the palm of his hand. Gerry appeared hypnotised by the motion.

"Out for a puck around, are ye?" he said, looking around at them all.

"Well, that depends," Francis said, tilting his head to one side. "I've had reports that you threatened my daughter."

"What?"

"You heard me. In broad daylight. You followed her and threatened her. Now." Francis stepped closer and leant forward so there was less than a foot between his face and Gerry's. "Consider this your first and last warning. If I ever get an inkling that you so much as *thought* about hurting her, I won't be using this hurley to hit a sliotar. Do you get me? You hurt my family and you've made an enemy of me for life. And you don't want me as an enemy, Gerard. Believe me. Are we clear?"

Gerry had turned pale at this point. He stared up at Francis with what looked like fear in his eyes. He was almost unrecognisable from Ballycashel's self-titled hard man. "I'm not trying to rise you, Mr McCabe, but I've no idea what you're talking about."

CHAPTER 23

"Ah here, Gerry," Marty said. "Don't make it worse for yourself by lying about it."

"I'm not."

Fiona stepped forward. "You are. You tried to grab me on Church Street. Don't try and deny it."

"I… what… I…"

"Now listen to me," Francis said. "If you so much as—"

"I wasn't trying to hurt her," Gerry said, looking like he was about to burst into tears at any moment. "Is that what ye think it was?"

"What, you're going to try and tell us you were asking for directions? God, Gerry. At least think of a better lie."

"Sure why would I ask you for directions and I living here my whole life?"

"I was being sarcastic," Fiona snapped.

"Ah," he said, his face relaxing and taking on a dreamy faraway look. "You're a funny woman alright, Fiona McCabe. Though I don't get what you're talking about half the time."

The McCabes shuffled awkwardly, not sure how to proceed after this strange turn in the conversation.

"Anyway," Francis said at last. "I think we're clear. In summary: hurt or threaten her in any way and you'll have us hounding you for the rest of your days."

"I wasn't trying to hurt her!" Gerry protested, sounding hurt.

"I don't want any excuses."

By now, Gerry looked like a scolded puppy. "I wanted to ask her out is all. Is that a crime? I'm sorry to have caused you such offence."

"What?" Fiona had to lean against the table behind her to keep from falling over.

"Don't make me say it again in front of all of them," Gerry muttered. "It's the truth. I saw you at the ice-cream shop and thought I'd come and chat to you. You're always talking to other people in the pub. I thought it might be nice for us to have a private chat."

Francis McCabe looked like he was going to roar with laughter. Behind the bar, Jimmy was listening intently with the look of a man who was getting ready to get on the phone and tell the whole town. Ballycashel had a highly organised unofficial calling tree system for gossip-worthy situations like this: all the neighbours would know before they even got home. Not that any of them minded: Fiona was the only one of her siblings who had been able to maintain a straight face. It wasn't hard for her: she was so horrified all she could do was stare blankly at him.

"But you came at me again after that. I left the Garda station and you ran at me. Shouted about how you were after me. You can't deny that!"

"Lookit!" Gerry cried, throwing his hands skyward. He was now the colour of canned beetroot. "If you're not interested would you at least have the decency to stop making a holy show of me?"

"Ah," she said, as the penny dropped. "You didn't mean *after* as in trying to kill me. You mean after as in…"

He nodded miserably, not looking in her eyes.

At that point, Ben and Marty lost the battle to maintain their composure. They howled with laughter, doubling over and clutching their sides.

***

"Good God, Fiona. No wonder you're single if you think young fellas are out to murder you when all they want to do is wine and dine you."

"Not now, Dad," Fiona muttered as they left the pub. "Slag me later, but not now. It's still particularly raw."

"So let me get this straight. Would you rather have him murder you than…" Ben asked with a smirk.

Fiona winced. "Shut up. Please. Or I'll take that cricket bat to you."

"Freeze!"

Sergeant Brennan was waiting at the side of the building with a megaphone in his hand and Gardas Fitzpatrick and Conway in tow.

"Ah. You've a lovely new toy I see, Sergeant," Francis McCabe said with a smirk.

"Put down your weapons!"

Francis frowned. "Weapons? What're you on about? These are hurleys."

"The hurleys!" Sergeant Brennan screeched.

They all winced as the megaphone crackled.

"Put them down," Fi hissed. "We don't know what he's capable of."

Marty shook his head. "That's what I've been trying to tell you all morning. No one would listen."

"Listen to what?"

"Put down your weapons! This is your last warning!"

"We got it all wrong. About Dec. We were too busy going after Gerry to discuss it."

Their father turned. "Throw them down lads, go on."

They did as he instructed and only then did Sergeant Brennan lower his megaphone and come closer to them. "What are you doing?"

"I told you, Sergeant Brennan," Mr McCabe said sounding weary. "We're out for a game of hurling."

"We've had reports of a mob stalking through the town."

Marty folded his arms. "Well, you'd better go and arrest them, hadn't you?"

"It's you," Sergeant Brennan said, eyes bulging, "that I've had the reports about."

"Reports from who?"

"From *whom*. And I have no requirement to tell you."

"Ah okay, fair enough. Can we go on and have our game now?"

"Why don't you drop the pretence? What's he doing with that cricket bat?"

Francis turned and stared at Ben as if seeing him for the first time. "Ah, sure he's always at that. Didn't he start supporting United as soon as they were winning years ago, and he got all into the rugby when Leinster got good? He got that yoke when Ireland won against England. I suppose that was a devastating blow for you."

Sergeant Brennan narrowed his eyes. "Why'd you say that?"

"I don't know," Francis countered. "You seem like the type who'd begrudge your own countrymen a victory."

Sergeant Brennan looked like he was about to blow a gasket. The two Gardaí stood behind him, grinning silently. "Come on. I'm going to have to arrest you all."

"Why?" Francis asked, looking mystified. "For playing hurling? Are you going to ban the tricolour next?"

"You're not playing hurling!" Sergeant Brennan bellowed. "Do you take me for a fool? I don't know what you're at, but it's not hurling. You don't even have a ball."

"What do you mean?" Fiona asked, reaching in her handbag. "Of course we do." She pulled out two sliotars and threw one each to her father and Marty, who caught them on their sticks. "We'd better go—it looks like rain and we don't want to be playing on soggy ground."

CHAPTER 24

"God almighty," Francis McCabe said, shaking his head as they watched Sergeant Brennan stalk away with his back ramrod straight. "That was the most fun I've had all year. What possessed you to bring the sliotars?"

She shrugged. "When I saw you weren't to be reasoned with, I thought the least I could do was provide some damage control."

"You had them in your bag the whole time."

She nodded. "I grabbed them as I ran after ye out the back door."

Marty placed a hand on each of their shoulders, his face grave. "You can congratulate yourselves later. We need to talk. *Now.*"

It was so rare for him to be serious that they all fell into line without question. Luckily, Fiona had the keys to the pub in her cavernous handbag so they headed there to talk.

"What is it?" Fiona asked nervously as she locked the inner door behind them. "It's the

Beetle isn't it? With all the Gerry business I didn't think to ask."

"Yeah, what is it?" Francis asked. "You're going to tell us now?" He turned to Fiona. "He refused to say a word until you got home."

"In fairness, I thought she deserved to hear about it before we all ran off half-cocked. And I was right—look at how much trouble we'd be in if she hadn't thought to bring the sliotars."

"What did you find, Marty?"

They sat around the large table opposite the bar. Three curious faces turned to him expectantly.

"I don't have it on me. I hid it at home because I didn't know what might come of our little venture into town."

Fiona felt panic grip her. "Is it safe? Where'd you put it? What if they come looking for it?"

He patted her shoulder. "It's fine. And it turns out that there's no *they.*"

"Pete was working alone? But I saw him at the Garda station."

"It wasn't Pete," Marty said with a sigh. "Dec left behind a diary of sorts. Emails, records. I was only able to glance through it, but it's pretty clear what went on. It appears Dec wasn't expecting things to escalate as much as they did. I think he used the car as a hiding place because Will wouldn't think to look there. He went to great lengths to get that land."

"Wait a sec. *Will* wouldn't find it? But Pete bought the land—or so he said."

Marty nodded. "It seems Will had been harassing Dec for years to sell him the land."

"But it wasn't his to sell. His parents are still in that home."

"That's what we all thought, but the deeds were in Dec's name. He spelt it all out. Will wanted it badly. Dec refused to even think about selling, but his time in jail made him rethink. He was thinking about getting out of Ballycashel for good. He decided to sell, but Pete Prendergast heard about it before they finalised the deal. He made a better offer for the land."

"No way," Fiona whispered. "I'd say Will must have been livid."

"He was. See, not only did Pete gazump him, but he's planning to build greenhouses on the land. It'll hurt Will financially as well as sentimentally."

"Why kill Dec then? Why not Pete?"

Marty shrugged. "I have no idea. All I found in there were the documents. There are records of Will's visits to his house; of the harassment. He'd been following him all around the town and he'd taken to sitting at the bar with him in Phelan's."

Fiona groaned. "That's why he was sticking to himself. It wasn't jail at all—he didn't want Will harassing him. No wonder Will started coming in then. I wondered: I'd never seen him in the pub before. So you don't think Robocop's involved? Why didn't he suspect Will?"

"There's no record of Dec making a statement about the harassment. That's understandable—he doesn't trust the guards after what they did."

"So what do we do now?" Ben asked. "We should take this to them."

"Yeah," Fiona admitted. "If they're not dirty, then they're the best ones to look into this. We could take it to Garda Fitzpatrick; bypass the sergeant."

"Good idea," Marty grinned. "I certainly don't think it's a good idea to try and sort this out ourselves. I've had quite enough McCabe vigilantism for one week."

"Good," Fiona said with a relieved sigh.

"Yeah, Fi; do us all a favour and learn to spot the signs for when a fella fancies you versus when he wants to murder you. Maybe we can make you a poster with stick men and speech bubbles."

"Har har har," Fiona said, rolling her eyes, but she couldn't keep the smile off her face. "It's a family of comedians I have."

CHAPTER 25

Declan Hanlon's dossier proved quite comprehensive. He'd kept records of emails and had made notes of every conversation he'd had with Pete Prendergast and Will Connolly. It was enough to arrest Will and charge him with Dec's murder. It transpired that the Gardaí had searched Will's property before and found nothing—the search was perfunctory and mainly because he was an apple producer. This time, his laptop was taken. Among his search history was recipes for poisons that could be produced from common ingredients and detailed instructions for how to prepare apple seeds in order to induce cyanide poisoning. They also discovered that Will was the one who had anonymously tipped the Gardaí off about Fiona's supposed involvement.

There had been a dispute between the Hanlon and Connolly families about that land for years. It all traced back to a distant relative of both men. That will was unclear and both families believed they were the rightful owners of the land. Will had heard all about the dispute as he grew up and it had come back to him as he grew older and began to look into his family history. He had become obsessed with getting his hands on it at all costs.

Declan had been fielding Will's offers for years. He'd been firmly against selling, but prison had given him a new perspective. His parents were in the nursing home and he had nothing left in the town. What did a piece of land matter? His records detailed his draft agreement with Will Connolly. They'd gone to the effort of visiting a solicitor to draft their sale agreement, though there was no public record of the document as the land had never been officially sold to Will.

One evening, Pete Prendergast approached Declan at his home and offered double what Will Connolly was offering. Declan didn't hesitate to accept. He had already decided to move to England, and as far as he was concerned he had no loyalty to either man. All he wanted was to build as big a nest egg as possible for his new life.

The resulting drama and recriminations were far more explosive than Declan had anticipated. He began to receive silent phone calls. His gates were left open and his sheep were allowed to escape. Will confronted him one night in Phelan's. Dec thought it would all blow over. He had an inherent distrust of the police so it never entered his head to go to them for help.

He had another idea, though. He got in touch with Simon Moriarty and told him all about the drama. Moriarty, to his surprise, thought it was great stuff. A real slice of life in rural Ireland with secrets and skeletons in the closet, he had said. Declan had printed off the email for posterity.

In the end, that turned out to be Declan's biggest mistake. Will saw him in the pub that night, lording it up with that journalist, as he put it in his statement to the Gardaí. He felt even more defeated by the man who had robbed him of what was rightfully his.

He had to act. He was a smart man; he had already researched poisons but talked himself down before taking action. Now there was no calming him. All he had to do was hurry home and double check exactly how many seeds were needed and he was in business. It didn't take him more than an hour to extract more seeds than he needed and mill them in a blender. He rushed back to the pub and waited around in the shadows, pretending he was just having a smoke outside.

He started to get antsy. He popped his head in the door quickly and established that Dec was still there. He went back to waiting, never once rethinking his plan. He'd been scorned; made a fool of. When Dec left the pub, it was only a matter of lying and telling him that he wanted to talk; that he'd been an awful eejit and he wanted to say sorry.

They went down to the lock and shared a beer. It would have all looked legit to Dec: Will had uncapped the bottled and recapped it after he put the apple seeds in. It turned out that he was an avid home brewer of beer, though he had no interest in going into the commercial business of cider production.

Pete Prendergast had been living in terror ever since Dec's murder. He had a suspicion, but he couldn't be sure. He'd thought the same as the rest of Ballycashel at first: Dec had been killed for something he'd found out in prison. It was only when the truth came out about the journalist and the cyanide that Pete realised just what had happened. Even then, though, he wasn't too worried about himself. After all, Will had never threatened to hurt him: only excavate the field so it'd be utterly useless to him. Pete had spent more than he could afford to buy the land: there was no way he could afford to pay for trucks to come and take the soil away. He had taken to patrolling the land with his shotgun, living in a small tent hidden in the bushes. It was the only way to guarantee its safety until the bank loan for construction came through and he could start work. He had avoided any contact with Will Connolly, fearing he might set off the other man's temper. He had planned a relaxed evening out with his wife assuming that Connolly would never choose a venue like McCabe's: it had put the fear of God into him when he'd spotted him at the bar.

That morning in the field had been the last straw. Pete had almost had a heart attack when he saw them approaching. He'd thought they were thugs hired by Connolly. He'd never felt so ashamed as he watched them hurry away, afraid that he was going to shoot them. He'd gone to see the Gardaí after that. What did it matter if Connolly retaliated? That land was a curse; it had destroyed his marriage and turned him into a madman who slept in a tent with a shotgun for company.

As for Mrs Flannery's shifty behaviour in the pub that night, Fiona had tried to approach the subject delicately but it was no use. Mrs Flannery had closed up the moment Moriarty's name was mentioned and Fiona hadn't wanted to upset her further. Speculation was rife in the McCabe household that she'd previously had a run-in with the journalist, though they couldn't think what might anger such a lovely, even-tempered woman.

CHAPTER 26

It took a few weeks for the excitement to die down around the town. Will Connolly's arrest brought a buzz to the place. Fiona felt sorry for his mother, who seemed to have been found guilty by association.

"Ara, it's understandable too," Mrs McCabe said as Fiona made them tea. "She's had an awful shock. I always thought there was something funny about that boy."

"So you've claimed."

It was funny—Mrs McCabe had only had good things to say about Will before he was identified as the murderer.

"I *did*," she protested.

Various complicated looks passed between her children, but no one said anything. It was too early in the morning for another argument.

They drank their tea and ate their breakfasts in silence—almost unheard of in the McCabe household. After all the excitement of the previous weeks, it seemed they all craved peace and calm.

Francis slapped his paper and shattered the silence. "Ah, would you look at this. Your man Simon Moriarty has a book coming out. He didn't waste any time."

"A book?"

"Oh yeah," Fi said. "Remember, he was writing that book about Dec's experience selling the land."

"I wouldn't have minded that so much. He's gone and revised his plan. See here." He dropped the paper and folded it quickly with the dexterity of a card shark. He passed it to Fiona who was sitting closest to him. Her eyes widened as she read.

"Greed and the re-emergence of the Celtic Tiger: how one man's wealth-seeking led to his murder. Coming in August."

"Ah, I don't believe it."

"Believe it, Mam," Fiona said with a grimace, passing her the paper. "Looks like someone's about to profit from the unfortunate affair."

"Ah, sure it was what Dec would've wanted."

"He only wanted the money so he could provide for his parents and get himself over to England."

Mrs McCabe grinned widely. It was obvious that she was up to something.

"What is it, Mam?"

Her mother shook her head. "Nothing at all."

"No, there definitely is. You only put on that high-pitched voice when you're trying to play innocent. What are you up to?"

"Nothing. I told you," she said, reaching for Ben's plate even though his breakfast was only half-finished. "I'd better start on the washing up. Who's helping me? Come on you useless lumps."

***

Fiona's first instinct was to reach for the buzzer under the bar. She paused when she saw the look on his face. It made her wish she had a trapdoor in the floor she could just disappear into: that was another benefit to having a more traditional pub complete with a cellar under the bar.

"How's it going, Gerry? What can I get you?"

He looked stony-faced. In fact, if Fiona hadn't heard him declare his feelings for her, she'd assume he was coming to murder her now. He certainly had a strange way of showing his emotions.

"I'm alright," he said, taking a seat at the bar.

Fiona thought about buzzing Marty in the hardware shop anyway just to avoid the awkwardness of this conversation, but she stopped herself. It had to happen sometime and it was better to get it out of the way.

"Ah, good stuff. You're sure I can't get you a drink?" She wanted to apologise for being responsible for him being hunted by a mob of McCabes, but she had no desire to be the first to bring it up.

She hadn't heard the end of it since it happened: even her mother had been giving her stick about Gerry and asking why she wouldn't give him a go. Her father had declared his intention to break Gerry's legs if he ever went near her, no matter what her feelings were.

In other words, the McCabe household had returned to normal.

"Here, I wanted to talk to you about that day. You know. With the ice-cream. And the hurleys."

"Yeah," she said, playing with her fingernails and trying to guess the exact shade of red her face had become. Beetroot or tomato? She focused on it as hard as she could as she willed him not to say what she felt sure he was about to say.

"Listen, I'm after realising we never had a chance to talk one-to-one with the... ah... mix-up."

"Yeah," she said. "That's true."

The cosmos must not have been listening to her, because he carried on without pausing. "I was wondering, Fiona, if you'd want to go out sometime. For a drink maybe, or to the cinema?"

Her composure left her. She didn't want to be cruel to him, but what was she supposed to say? She wouldn't go out with him because he was the town scumbag and he was still wearing the same neon-stripe Adidas tracksuit bottoms that everyone else in the town had stopped wearing back in nineteen ninety eight?

So she did what she always did when she felt rushed or panicked. "Ah listen, Gerry, I can't. It's not possible," she babbled. "I've a boyfriend. It's only new but I think he's the one. Sorry about that."

He stared at her, frowning. "I didn't know that. I would have heard."

She shrugged. "I don't know."

"I would have. You know how fast news travels around here. What's his name?"

Fiona swallowed. As much as she babbled when she was under pressure, she wasn't great at making up lies on the spot. "Felix," she said quickly.

"Felix?" Gerry repeated, as if he'd never come across the name before. "What kind of a name is that?"

"Oh, he's… German. You know, from Germany."

"And what's he doing over here?" Gerry folded his arms and leant his elbows on the bar. "I've never seen a German around Ballycashel."

"Oh you wouldn't have known," she said quickly. "His job relies on him blending in. It's for his own safety."

"Why? What does he do?"

"He's in the army."

"But sure," Gerry said with a frown. "The German army doesn't operate over here. Does he live in Germany?"

"No, no," Fiona said, shaking her head as she tried to collect her thoughts. She couldn't back out now. "He's in the Irish army. See, that's why he has to blend in. If they found out he was a German…"

"They'd what?"

She shrugged. "I don't know. That's the thing. He won't tell me. But there'd be serious consequences for him."

"Like getting him deported back to Germany?"

"Maybe." She made a big show of wiping her eyes. "Don't. I can't even think about that. It'd break my heart."

Gerry studied her for a while. "When's he coming here next?"

She stared at him. "What?"

"When's he coming to visit you?"

Fiona had the familiar feeling that she'd bitten off more than she could chew. "I don't know yet.

He's very busy. Next week or the week after, probably."

"And will he be in here?"

"I don't know, Gerry. I don't have a crystal ball, do I?"

"I'm only asking." He was silent for a while. "I've never met a German. I'd like to see him. I'm curious."

Me too, Fiona thought. Instead, she smiled as patiently as she could. "Yeah, he's a great guy."

"I'm sure he is," Gerry said gruffly.

CHAPTER 27

"Oh God," Fiona said as she came in the door and pulled out her usual chair at the table. "You'll never guess what happened last night." She looked around. "Where's Mam?"

Kate and Ben were sitting on the other side of the long table, and Marty was sitting at one end. All of then shrugged. "What happened last night?"

Fiona wasn't sure if she could even bring herself to repeat the story out loud. "Do any of ye know any Germans?"

Ben looked at her with a frown. "Michael Schumacher?"

"No, I meant—"

"Michael Fassbender," Kate offered.

"Is he not from Kerry?"

"Germany originally."

"Are you serious?" Ben asked. "But the accent on him. How can he be German?"

"Lads!" Fiona said, holding up her hands. "Stop. Listen. I meant do you know any Germans *personally*? Not off the telly or the movies or whatever."

"Fi, this is Ballycashel."

"I'm well aware of that."

"So you'll be aware too that the foreign population is pretty minimal. We're not exactly twin cities with Dusseldorf, are we?"

She buried her head in her hands. "Oh God, what have I done?"

This, of course, only fed their curiosity. "What happened? What's going on?"

She groaned. "Gerry came into the pub last night to ask me out. I panicked and said I had a boyfriend. A German boyfriend called Felix."

"Why on earth did you do that?"

"Well, I wasn't exactly going to tell him I wasn't interested in him and to leave me alone, was I? He'd probably steal my car and burn it out."

"Obviously," Kate said tossing her hair over her shoulder. "But why the hell would you say your man was German? Why not from Dublin or Belfast or somewhere?"

"I don't know," Fiona said mournfully. "I just don't know."

"You're some eejit," Marty said, shaking his head. "Where on earth are you going to find a German?"

"How about Germany?" Ben smirked.

"Very smart," Fiona said with a grin. "Pity you couldn't tap into that wisdom when you were doing your Leaving."

"Now you sound like Mam," Ben said, poking out his tongue.

"I do, don't I," Fi said. "Where is she? It's not like her to abandon her growing manchildren without feeding them full of breakfast first. Have ye seen her this morning?"

"We have, yeah. She was faffing around in here before."

"What's she at?"

Their only response was to shrug.

Fiona stood. "I'll go find her; see if she's alright."

She got as far as the kitchen door when her attention was caught by the radio. She stopped and stared at it, wondering if her mind was playing tricks on her.

"Lads," she said, turning around and gesturing at the radio. "This woman sounds identical to Mam. It's weird." She reached for the dial and turned up the volume.

They looked at her, half-interested. Then there was an ear-splitting moment of static interference.

"God, Fi, turn it down. It's like listening to nails on a blackboard."

Fiona reached for the dial just as the radio presenter said "there seemed to be a radio in the background there. Can I get you to turn it down?"

"Ah, sorry Joe," that uncannily familiar voice said. "One of the kids must have messed with it. I'll just go sort it now."

To Fiona's astonishment, her mother emerged from the hall a couple of seconds later.

"Stop messing with that," she said, swatting Fi's hand away.

"What are you up to, Mam? Are you on the radio?"

But Mrs McCabe was gone again and she didn't bother to answer. Fiona gestured for the others to come closer. This time they showed more interest.

"You're back, Mrs McCabe."

"I am." There was a coquettish air to her voice that they had heard when she'd called Simon Moriarty.

"And you were telling me about a terrible story down there in Bally… Bally…"

"Ballycashel."

"Ah yes. A lovely spot. Why don't you tell us what went on."

"Well," Mrs McCabe said. "There was a murder. A terrible affair. The long and the short of it is it was a property deal gone sour. The poor young lad who was killed only sold the bit of land to get some money together to pay for the nursing home for his parents."

"Ah God," the presenter said in his enunciated radio voice. "That's awful. I hope they got the fellas who did it."

"Oh yes," Mrs McCabe said disapprovingly. "They did."

Fiona pictured her mother fighting hard not to slate the Gardaí in Ballycashel. She knew it must have been hard. "What's she doing? What's the point in calling Joe?" she hissed.

"Maybe she's lonely."

"But she has all of us."

"Anyway, Joe, as terrible as that is, there's another part to the story. More greed, if you like. You see, this poor young fella thought that the scandal of it might help with his savings. He got in touch with a journalist and told him the story, you know, on the proviso that the profits would be shared."

"And what happened there, Margaret?"

"Well the poor boy is gone and your man gets to keep all the profits to the book!"

Fiona rubbed her face and stared in disbelief. "She didn't."

"It looks like she did," Marty said with a grin. "Fair play to her."

"Her and her pet causes. I swear she makes those environmental activists look like a lazy bunch of schoolkids."

"Shh," Fiona said.

The presenter was addressing his listeners now, telling them the background and referring to the book. When he wrapped it up, he hit them with the twist.

"We have Simon Moriarty on the other line."

All four of them gasped. They could hear their mother's cry of surprise from two rooms away. "Oh no," Fiona groaned. "She's going to get herself sued for slander."

"Would ye shush?" Ben said. "I'm trying to listen to this."

They all fell silent and listened with growing amazement. Because it soon became clear that their mother wasn't going to be sued. In fact, it looked like she might just have gotten her way by shaming Simon Moriarty on national talk radio, the heartland of his fans.

"I'll be splitting the royalties with the Hanlon family in light of this. Thank you for bringing it to my attention, Mrs McCabe."

All four siblings whooped. Sure it was only money, but it felt like a victory. At least Declan's actions might result in something positive for his parents.

CHAPTER 28

Fiona glanced anxiously as the door to the pub opened. "Right, Angus, this might be him. Remember what you've to do?"

"I thought my name was Felix."

"It is," she hissed, before turning and pretending to wipe down the fridges.

"Howaya Fiona."

She turned and looked up, even though she had known immediately who the voice belonged to. "Oh, hi Gerry. How's it going?"

"Can't complain," he said, looking around.

"Just thought you'd pop in for a drink, did you?"

He nodded. "Thirsty work this afternoon."

Fiona knew well that the only reason he was there was one of his buddies had told him about the tall fella who'd been spotted going into McCabe's. As if to confirm that, Gerry was now staring down her brother Colm's college friend.

"I haven't seen you around here before, buddy."

Angus/Felix shook his head. "*Ja,*" he said in the most terrible German accent Fiona had ever heard. "I am not from *diese* town."

Fiona cringed but it was too late to intervene. Colm had suggested Angus because he'd been a keen amateur dramatist when the two were in college. He had been badgering Colm for months to take him out fishing, so a deal had been struck. She hadn't banked on his hammy acting: she just hoped Gerry wouldn't notice.

"That's quite an accent there. Where's that from?"

"München."

"Where's that now?"

"It eez in Germany."

"Ah," Gerry said, feigning astonishment and making Angus's acting seem Oscar-worthy. "I see. You're the boyfriend so," he said, nodding at Fiona.

"I am ze boyfriend of Fiona. Ja. Yes." Angus nodded vigorously and Fiona wished there was a way for her to kick him under the bar, or to scream *enough* without Gerry hearing.

Gerry looked him up and down, sizing him up for the third time. She tapped the buzzer under the bar four times; short fast bursts. It was the signal that Gerry was on the premises. She doubted he'd kick off, but she didn't want Angus getting a black eye because he'd been kind enough to help her out.

"What can I get for you, Gerry?"

He stared up at the menu. He had stopped the 'Guinness' routine soon after she told him she was taken. She had realised—to her horror—that far from being a wind-up, it was what he considered a chatup line. She certainly wasn't confident about the future state of her love life if that was the general level of charm possessed by Ballycashel men.

"I'll have one of those ciders."

"Coming up."

"What are you drinking, pal?"

Fair play to Angus, he had insisted on ordering a German wheat beer to get in character. As far as Fiona knew, his only exposure to Germany had come from a weekend visiting a friend who was doing an Erasmus exchange years ago.

"It is a German Weissbier."

"Good stuff. Actually, you know what? I'll try one of them, Fiona."

"Coming right up," she said, turning to get it from the fridge. "Do you want the same again, darling?"

"Yes please, Sugar dumpling."

"Sugar dumpling," Gerry repeated. He sighed. "Here, hold that beer. I just remembered some work I was supposed to do."

"Ah, right so. No problem, Gerry."

Fiona didn't trust herself to turn around until he was gone. She turned and her eyes met Angus's. They both burst into laughter. Luckily, the bar was empty apart from them.

"Thanks so much for that," Fiona said when she had gotten her breath back.

"No worries at all," Angus said, swiping his hand through the air. "Anything for Colm. Plus it finally got him to agree to take me out fishing."

"You've never been?"

He shook his head. "Never. There wasn't much opportunity in the middle of the city and I'd no interest in catching a shopping trolley or someone's old boot."

Fiona laughed. "I suppose not."

"Will you join us?"

Fiona grimaced. "I prefer to think of fish coming from a fish tree rather than being caught with… you know…" She'd been fishing a grand total of twice as a child, and the experience had turned her off fish for years.

"Fair enough," he laughed. "I've never done it, but I suppose catching worms isn't everyone's cup of tea. I'll bait your line for you, how's about that?"

She smiled. Oddly enough, it didn't seem like such an off-putting prospect after all. "We'll see," she said. "Will you gut whatever I catch as well?"

He pretended to think about it. She waited, watching him closely until he finally nodded. "I suppose. Sure what's the harm?"

The bell over the door rang and Fiona turned dreamily to see who it was. The sight of her brother Colm gave her a jolt of unease: he never missed an opportunity to tease her. Sure enough, his face broke into a wide smile when he saw it was just the two of them.

"Aha, what do we have here?" he said, easing himself onto a bar stool and looking puzzled. "Is Gerry hiding out the back?"

Fiona shook her head, knowing where he was going and struggling to stop herself laughing out of sheer mortification. "Nope."

"But ye two are looking very cosy altogether. What's that about?"

Fiona turned to wipe down the fridges before they could see her flush. "We're just getting into character."

"That's it," Angus said enthusiastically. "Method actors."

"Method my foot," Colm said, roaring with laughter. "The moony eyes on the pair of you."

Fiona spun around. "I see Lourdes hasn't improved you anyway."

Colm rolled his eyes. "I'm only having the craic with you. Anyway, how on earth did you think Lourdes would improve me?"

She shrugged. "I don't know. It's a religious place, isn't it? Didn't you go there on a pilgrimage?"

She was surprised when he laughed even harder than before.

"What's so funny?"

He shook his head in seeming disbelief. "A pilgrimage? You think that's why Granny goes there every year?"

"Yeah," she said frowning. "You know that. She's been going every year since we were kids."

"She has," he said, standing again and coming around the side of the bar to help himself to a cider. "Well, it's not praying she's doing over there, that's for sure."

"What then? Here, you can pay me for that—just for being such a funny man when you came in."

He reached into his pocket and pulled out a fiver. "We were amazed too, to be honest. It turns out it's all just a big jolly for them. They spent more time playing cards and betting than they did in the churches. I'm telling you…"

Fiona sighed. It might have been hard to believe of anyone else, but anything was possible with her family.

THE NEXT FIONA MCCABE MYSTERY IS COMING SOON:

Fiona had literally only taken her finger off the buzzer under the bar when the phone rang.

"McCabe's."

"Fi, it's Ben."

She frowned. "Hold on, Ben. Are you ringing about the buzzer? It's grand. I thought Marty was working there—I was only buzzing him to come over for a cuppa. It's quiet here."

Ben had recently—and reluctantly—started working at the hardware shop. Fiona tried not to give him an excuse to skive off: he'd close up the shop for the whole afternoon and sit in the pub drinking if she gave him the chance.

She was about to hang up when he yelled her name again.

"It's all good, Ben. It wasn't an emergency buzz. To be honest, we mainly use it as a tea signal—aside from all the madness after the time Dec was murdered. Thanks for ringing, though. How's everything going in the shop?"

"How the hell should I know?"

She sighed. Ben hadn't inherited the same work ethic as the rest of them and sometimes it grated on her. "There's no need to sound so enthusiastic. You should be grateful to have the job."

"I am," he gasped. "Of course I am. But I have no idea how the shop is. I'm not rostered to work again until Thursday."

Fiona frowned and shook her head. "That's really funny, Ben. I just buzzed Marty for tea and you rang a second later. I honestly thought—"

"Fi!"

She finally became aware of the panic in his voice. Fiona's jaw clenched. She'd never heard Ben sound so stressed before. "What is it, Ben? What's happened?"

He gasped and she pictured him pacing around the hall at home, panicked out of his mind.

"Please, Ben. Tell me what's wrong."

"It's Mam," he hissed. "She's been arrested. You've got to come quickly. I don't know what to do."

"What?" she laughed. The idea of her mother being arrested was utterly ridiculous. "You seriously think you can fool me that easily?"

"Ben?" she asked when he didn't respond.

"Fiona, just come home. They're just after taking her."

"Who's after taking her?"

Ben sniffed. "All of them. Garda Fitzpatrick and Conway and Robocop. Smirking away he was."

"But why?" Fiona asked. "The woman keeps to laws that don't even exist in Ireland. What could she possibly have done?"

Then she heard the dial tone. He'd hung up. There was no mistaking the panic in his voice—this was no joke.

"Oh good God," she cried, reaching for her keys and phone. "What's after happening now?"

The door opened just as she was running out from behind the bar.

"Where are you off to?" Marty asked, smiling. "I thought you buzzed me for a cuppa. It's awful quiet in the shop—I wish they'd put on a new DIY show on the telly. That always gets them out—"

"Come on," Fiona interrupted, grabbing his arm and hurrying towards the door. "We've got to go!"

80027374R00144

Made in the USA
San Bernardino, CA
21 June 2018